Interludes - The Collection

INTERLUDES

INTERLUDES II

INTERLUDES III

MELISSA

PAIGE

ANNA ELLIS
THREE BIRDS PRESS

Contents

Interludes

Anna Ellis

Three Birds Press

Contents

Emma

"WE JUST WAIT AROUND and let Tia pick who we get?" I ask Jacey in disbelief. "How can that work?"

We're at Tia's on a Saturday night. I'm at my first key party where apparently I will be havi sex with one of the neighbours. He'll be selected for me.

I can't believe I'm doing this.

"It just works. Tia runs the show." Jacey pops an olive in her mouth and I hand her a napkin.

"*She's* the only one who has these things? These parties, I mean? Why does she get to pick?" I glance over to where Tia is laughing with a few of the husbands. She's a beautiful woman; at least fifteen years older than I am, but still amazing looking.

She intimidates me.

There's something about her – the way she moves, the way she carries herself. Sensuality. Tia is a very sensual woman and I am not and that is one of the few things that intimidate me.

Jacey shrugs. "It's her party. You didn't have to come."

I close my eyes briefly. Jacey has the same air of sensuality as Tia does. You can just tell she's into sex and very good at it. I wonder if Tia and Jacey have ever been together. I wonder if women get together at these parties. I quickly count the guests – there is an extra woman. Does that mean...?

I can't do that. I'm not ready for that.

I'm out of my comfort zone here and I don't like it. Technically it was my decision to come to this party with our new neighbours. The neighbours seemed so normal and nice and so friendly when we moved in but under the surface, they had some sort of kinky and perverse swinging game going on with each other.

As soon as I heard about the parties at Tia's, I knew it would be something Nathan would want to try. It's not like Nathan is kinky or perverse or anything, but I know I'm not giving him what he wants in the bedroom. I'm just not that good at sex. There is no air of sensuality to me.

I should correct that; it's not that I'm *bad*, I'm just not that comfortable with the act. Despite being in love with Nathan and still so attracted to him, it comes down to the fact that I really don't think I *like* sex. Or I'm not experienced enough to decide if I like it.

Sex has never been that important to me. Coming to the party is my attempt to spice things up in the bedroom, as unorthodox as that seems. If I can learn to like sex, then Nathan will be happier. Things are fine with Nathan and me in that regard, but sex has never been the earth-shattering event described in books. And I know it's not Nathan's fault because he's willing to try anything with me. He *wants* to try everything, even some things I've never heard about.

He'd love to see me with another woman.

Sex was such a taboo subject when I was growing up that it still makes me hesitant when it comes to experimentation. I've never felt the need to explore, experiment or add a little variety or spice to things. I married Nathan fully expecting him to be the only and last man I would ever sleep with.

Apparently, I was wrong.

Nathan and I are here at Tia's, at this *key party* or whatever they call it, and I'm waiting for Tia to pick the man I'm going to have sex with.

I look over at Jacey beside me. "When does it start?"

"Soon. Just relax and have fun. You'll have fun," she assures me.

"I hope you're right."

She smiles at me. I don't know Jacey very well yet, but I can tell she's not a big smiley person, so the sight of it does reassure me. "Trust me. It'll be Mahak and he'll take *very* good care of you. That tongue..."

What's all this about his tongue?

I mean, I do know what a man does to a woman with his tongue because Nathan has tried it on several occasions, but it's not for me. It was nice, but it comes down to the fact I can't relax enough to really enjoy it.

I've had a total of three orgasms in my life.

"I need more wine," I tell Jacey.

"I could go for a refill too," she agrees and leads me to the bottle on the table.

Jacey is married to Dominic, who is so nice and cute and they seem happy together. I know they are happy in the bedroom because Nathan convinced me to spy on them from our bedroom window. It was only one time but it was kind of exciting watching them having sex. It was something I've never done before, never even thought of doing.

One of those three orgasms happened after we watched them, but I'm not about to send a thank you card to Jacey and Dominic for their help.

But even with Jacey obviously having amazing sex – at least how it looked to me – with her nice and very cute husband, I know she still has something going on with the guy in the car. I can't be positive but I think it's Mahak, who is married to Melissa. I've made it a point to remember all of the names of the couples and their children. I used to be a substitute teacher, so remembering names has always been easy for me.

Mahak, who Jacey tells me, will be my date for the evening.

Date sounds wrong. It's not like he's going to wine and dine me. We'll be having a tryst. A rendezvous. An assignation. An interlude.

Sex. That's all it is. No big deal. It'll be fun.

I'm going to have sex with my neighbour.

My new neighbours like to have sex with each other. I think this makes them swingers. I look around the room where everyone is talking and laughing and having fun together. *They* can relax and enjoy themselves.

I drain my second glass of wine to help my nerves.

"Mahak is married to Melissa," I say aloud. "And she's the one with the fake boobs."

Jacey laughs with a mouthful of wine and has a problem not spitting it out.

"I don't think she knows it's that obvious."

"It is. With her body type—and she does have an amazing body—she should be a B-cup, no more. Like me."

Jacey glances at my chest. "Your breasts look fine."

"Oh, I know. But compared to you they're on the small side." Now it's my turn to check out her measurements. "They're real?"

Jacey actually puts a hand on one of her breasts with another smile. "All mine."

"Lovely," I tell her.

"Thanks."

Not only am I at a swingers' party, but I'm also now comparing breast sizes with another woman. What has gotten into me?

"Colin is married to Paige," I continue.

"She's great," Jacey says quickly.

"She seems nice but I get the impression there's always an inside joke going on with her. I haven't spoken to Colin yet, so I hope I don't end up with him. I would like to have had at least a conversation with the man before I go off for our interlude."

"Interlude?"

"What do you call it?" I ask curiously.

Jacey looks perplexed. "Sex? A casual encounter with a neighbour *slash* friend which will result in the two of us enjoying coitus?"

"You actually call it coitus?"

"You seem to want to look at the procedural aspects of this. Is intercourse more to your liking?"

"I think so." Now that the terms have been clarified, I turn my attention back to the party-goers. "Now, Wendy is married to Jackson. He seems like a player."

"Jackson?" Jacey laughs. "I'm not sure I'd call him that but he does enjoy this arrangement. He likes our interludes. Not just with me," she hastens to add. "Although I don't think the men really talk about what goes on with us."

"Do the wives?"

"Melissa wants to. I think they used to, but I'm not one for kissing and telling, so I think that put a damper on her tales. Melissa would critique, from what I heard. I'm not into that."

"I wouldn't be either. I can't imagine discussing this with anyone."

Jacey glances shyly at me. "Well, we've all gone through this, so if you need to have a discussion, you know where I am." She says this awkwardly like she's not used to making a gesture of friendship. If that's what it was.

"Thanks," I tell her sincerely. "So what's the story with Tia?"

"Tia is a...she's a mystery to us all," Jacey says admiringly. "She's something else."

I don't want to know what she means by that because Tia is starting to pull keys from the crystal bowl...

"Oh, god, is she starting?" I cry.

The others had drifted closer while Jacey and I were talking and I was overheard by all.

Mahak looks over at me with his dark eyes and I feel a lurch in my belly. "Excited already, my dear? It's always so much fun the first time."

Nathan moves beside me and grips my hand. "Are you sure about this?" he asks urgently. Nathan refused the invitation at first, certain that I only agreed to the idea because of him. But he forgot how persistent and stubborn I can be. It didn't take me long to convince him swinging with the neighbours was something I wanted to try as well, which proved to me that really wanted to try it.

I attempt to smile at my husband even though my heart is hammering with what can only be described as fear. I love him so much. All I want to do is to make him happy and if having sex with another man will somehow help... "Yes," I say as firmly as I can, even though I wish we could run out of here before anything else happens.

But the moment of escape quickly passes when Nathan pulls me close instead of pulling me out of there.

"I love you." Nathan drops a kiss on my forehead.

"I love you, too. This will be fun," I assure him, echoing Jacey's earlier words. Or am I just reassuring myself?

Nathan and I turn to watch Tia and her crystal bowl. She calls my name and I hold my breath. Will it be Mahak? Or Jackson? Dominic?

Jacey is right. Tia pulls out keys belonging to Mahak.

I'm going to have sex with Mahak.

He comes over to where I'm standing with Jacey and Nathan gives my hand a last squeeze and steps back. "Ladies," Mahak says in his deep and accented voice. He's the same height as Nathan, but my husband has broader shoulders.

I shouldn't be comparing them. Mahak is brutally attractive in the stereotypical tall, dark and handsome way. His eyes seem to bore right through me. I manage a weak smile and tell myself to breathe.

"Hello, Mahak," Jacey says. She leans over and gives him a kiss on the lips. "Be nice to Emma tonight, please."

"Aren't I always nice?" Mahak turns to me, all soulful eyes and a hungry smile. "I'm honoured to be your first. I'll do everything in my power to make it an enjoyable experience for you."

"I'm sure he will," Jacey smirks. "My turn now."

Tia has picked up Nathan's keys for Jacey.

I'm faced with a myriad of emotions, none of which I can put into words as I watch Jacey stand beside my husband. Nathan is staring at her with a mixture of fear and excitement. He turns to me with a final questioning look in his eyes.

This is my last chance to back out. Just a shake of my head and I can get out of here...

"Ready?" Mahak asks in a low voice.

I give Nathan the biggest smile I can manage and nod my consent. "As I'll ever be," I mutter to Mahak.

"There's no need to be nervous," Mahak tells me, slipping a hand around my waist to escort me out of the living room. He's so much taller than I am that he's leaning over me, cocooning me in his arms. "I'll be very gentle."

I meet his eyes, feeling more than a flutter of anticipation. And – could it be – excitement?

"Only if you want me to be," he adds.

I stop myself from glancing over my shoulder at Nathan.

Mahak leads me to a room in the basement, which seems like the longest walk I've ever taken.

"How long has this...thing... been going on?" I ask him. "The swinging, I guess you call it."

"I call it enjoying each other's company. It's been a few years," he answers evasively.

"Does everyone get their own room?" I ask as he shuts the door behind us.

"Of course. It's very private."

"But how do you know what room to take? Are they assigned? Is it first come, first –"

Mahak places a finger on my lips. "No more talking now. No more nerves."

"I can't help it," I confess. "I can't believe I'm doing this."

"Soon you'll be wondering when you can do it again."

"I like your accent," I whisper, as Mahak slides his arms around my waist. I should keep talking because if I keep talking then he won't kiss me.

But I want him to kiss me, don't I? Those full lips pressing down on my mouth. He'll be gentle but firm...

"I like your body," he tells me, running his hands up my back, leaving goosebumps in his wake. I shiver slightly at his touch, which develops into a trembling that I can't stop. "You mustn't be afraid."

"I'm not afraid," I tell him breathlessly. I feel like I'm sinking into those deep brown eyes and I have to shut my eyes before I drown. His scent surrounds me – spicy, exotic and very, very male.

He's not Nathan. Mahak is so different from Nathan. His smell, his breathing...the way he touches me...

His hand is on my shoulder, thumb sliding under the fabric of my dress and he is gently pushing it aside. His mouth...his lips...his tongue...

Mahak licks my shoulder and I feel a jolt between my legs. His hands stroke my back, and my shoulders, moving gently down to my bottom. But his mouth remains where it is, kissing my shoulder, over to my neck. His mouth is open and my breath catches at the feel of slow, measured licks of his tongue. My head falls to the side to give him more access to the sensitive skin.

Mahak covers my neck with his lips and his tongue, so distracting that I don't realize he has slid his hand under my dress until he's cupping my ass with only the slip of my panties between his hand and my bare skin.

His hand is warm. His mouth is hot. I'm about to overheat, especially when he licks my earlobe, sucking it between his lips. A whimper escapes, to my utter embarrassment, and sends his mouth back to my shoulder.

He takes a handful of my hair so that I'm looking up at him, not his hand. I'm having a hard time concentrating on anything but how warm his hand is, and how the material of my dress isn't thin enough. "I want you to enjoy this."

I manage to nod before his lips find mine.

Oh my.

I've only been kissed a few times by anyone other than Nathan. For the first time, I wondered what I've been missing. Mahak kisses are gentle at first, waiting until I part my lips under his. And then he deepens the kiss, darting his tongue inside my mouth, waiting until I tentatively touch it with my own. He slips a hand around the small of my back and draws me into him so my body moulds to his; so warm and smells so good. He releases my hair and his fingers begin a trail from my shoulder down my arm, sending trembling shivers racing through my body.

I could be happy to stand kissing him all night.

But I haven't been able to bring myself to touch Mahak yet. I don't know *how* to touch him. Should I put my arms around his neck? That feels high school-ish and teenager-y. What about hands on hips? All I can think about is his lips on mine and his hands which are now stroking my back. My knees feel weak like I should lean against something.

Before I can make a decision, Mahak's hands find the tie for my pink halter dress. Still, without moving his mouth from mine, he sweeps my hair to the side and slowly unknots it. I'm unable to move or catch the dress as it begins to slide down, checked by my body pressed firmly against his.

As Mahak pulls back, my dress falls to a puddle on the floor, and I'm standing before Mahak wearing only my thong. Instinctively, I cover my breasts with shaking hands but Mahak pulls them over my head, leaving me wide open for his admiring gaze.

"Beautiful," he murmurs. "So, so beautiful. Are you cold?" he asks, noticing the goosebumps on my stomach.

I'm sure he's noticed how tight my nipples are as well.

"N-no," I stammer.

"Is it because I'm touching you?" He sweeps his hand down the side of my body, before draping my arms around his neck.

"Yes," I admit with my head bowed.

He tips up my chin with a finger and kisses me gently on the lips. "No need to be shy."

"I've never done anything like this before," I confess.

"I know," he says, with an expression similar to a lion stalking his prey. I'm the prey. "That's why it's so exciting. For both of us." His fingers move lower to my legs, sending a trail of shivers up and down my hips. Then he suddenly tucks his hands around my bum and lifts me up. My legs automatically part and twine around his waist, my arms tightening around his neck.

"What are you doing?" I ask breathlessly.

Mahak's answer is to carry me to the bed in the centre of the room.

I had managed to ignore the bed in the room until I'm lying in the middle and Mahak smoothes my hair away from my face. He slides my thong down my legs with strong fingers and tosses it to the floor.

"Beautiful," he says again, caressing my breast. His fingers are gentle as if I'm a delicate fruit, before running his thumb across my nipple, erect and rosy pink. He holds my gaze the entire time, which I find awkward. I want to hide my face in the pillows instead of watching how one of his hands travels from one breast to the next, his other hand softly stroking my stomach.

I can't hide. I agreed to this. This is what I wanted.

Slowly, slowly, I feel myself begin to relax.

Mahak leans over and touches my breast with his mouth and I catch my breath. I don't realize I've gripped his shoulder with my hand until Mahak moves it to the nape of his neck. I can feel his thick curls and flex my fingers, inching slowly into the softness. He begins to kiss my breast, moving in circles, coming closer to the sensitive skin of my aureole. I can feel his breath against my nipple and press my hand against the back of his head in a wordless request for more.

He obeys; his mouth covering my nipple, drawing it gently between his lips and my breath escapes in a gasp. He swirls his tongue around the delicate area, laving it gently before sucking. I can feel his hand cupping my other breast, his thumb toying with the nipple. His other hand is resting on my inner thigh.

I must have spread them open because his hand drops between my legs and his fingers brush against my pussy.

His mouth finds my other breast, his tongue trailing between my cleavage as he moves across. By now my hand is clenched in Mahak's curls and I can hear my ragged breathing in the quiet room. My body is torn between the touch of his mouth and the new pressure between my legs as Mahak begins to stroke me with gentle fingers. I can feel my wetness as his finger probes between my lips and I part my legs wider. He nudges my clit and I gasp again, his mouth widening to a smile on my breast.

Then with a scrape of his teeth against my nipple, he stops.

I lay wide-eyed on the bed, trying to catch my breath as Mahak begins to undress. I can't believe I've become so aroused, managing to relax under his gentle touch, so much that I'm excited about what's to come.

Mahak's fingers fly through the buttons of his shirt and it falls to the floor. His leather belt slides through his pants and he folds it, slapping it gently against his palm as he looks at me with a raised eyebrow, laughing at my fearful expression.

"Not tonight," he assures me.

I can only stare at him as he continues to undress. I haven't seen many men with better bodies than Nathan but Mahak comes close. My eyes widen as he takes off his pants. The bulge in the front of his underwear...

He's too big. There's no way...

I shouldn't be doing this. This is *wrong*, this is my marriage. How can I be doing this?

I make a move to get off the bed just as a naked Mahak kneels on the bed beside me. I tense as he grasps my waist.

"So tiny," he murmurs. "No more nerves".

"I can't," I beg.

"You can. I only want to give you pleasure," he assures me. "Like Nathan will be doing for Jacey."

The mention of Nathan calms me. This is for my husband. This is what he wants – for both of us.

Mahak still holds me. "Shall I force you?" Mahak asks in a low voice. "You wouldn't be able to do anything to stop me."

My eyes widen.

"I could tie you up," he continues. "You might enjoy it like that. Then I could have my way with you, and you couldn't resist."

My breath catches at his suggestion. Nathan has never suggested something like that. I give a little nod and Mahak's eyes gleam.

He rummages in the nightstand drawer to find two silk ties. I'm glad they're vivid blue and purple, not gray. I haven't read those books but I know recreating some infamous scene is not something I'd enjoy.

At least not tonight. I never thought I'd be up to being tied up either.

Taking both of my wrists in his hand, Mahak pulls them above my head and runs his other hand possessively down my body.

I'm not sure how it's possible to both shy away from a touch and lean into it.

He rubs his thumb across my nipple, tight and hard from his mouth, and as he touches it, it's like a string attached to between my legs. He cups my other breast in his hand, again with his thumb rubbing the nipple as he leans over and licks it, twirling his tongue around the sensitive skin. Just as I'm beginning to enjoy his touch, Mahak reaches up and quickly ties one of my hands to the wrought-iron headboard.

"All right? Not too tight?"

"No," I whisper, still unable to believe I've agreed to this but quickly becoming unbearably excited. Mahak ties my other wrist and there I am, lying on the huge bed, my arms stretched uncomfortably but not painfully above my head and unable to move away from him.

From his hands roaming over my body like he has every right to.

I have absolutely no control over the situation.

Mahak returns to my breasts, kissing, stroking and caressing as I fight to control my breathing and struggle to control the urge to yank free of my restraints.

But why do I want to? Isn't this what I wanted? I need to relax and let go of my ever-need for control. I've given Mahak permission to do whatever he wants me with. I have to trust him.

I hardly know him. How can I trust him?

No choice now; his hands are dipping between my thighs, pushing them wide.

And then he begins to kiss his way down my stomach.

"I'm going to give you oral pleasure," Mahak tells me softly and I stiffen, immediately pulling my legs closed. A tiny moan escapes me and he tugs my legs open again.

"No," I whisper, squirming away from his hands.

Mahak chuckles. "You're playing the game. You must resist because you can do nothing to stop me."

"I'm not - " I begin, as he reaches between my legs with long fingers.

"I'm going to touch you right here. I'm going to taste you."

Only Nathan has ever touched me there. And now Mahak. Part of me can't wait, but the other part, the hesitant, fearful, *sexiswrong* part seems to be gaining momentum.

"Wait..." I try, but Mahak gives a commanding shake of his head.

His finger slips between my lips into my wetness. I whimper a bit and try futilely to close my legs but Mahak crouches between them. He takes my legs in his hands, spreading and pushing them towards my chest. "I'm going to make you come. I'm going to make you scream and beg for more."

And I feel his mouth.

I cry out as soon as I feel his tongue; out of fear, out of embarrassment, out of anger that he didn't stop when I wanted him to. Why did I agree to be tied up? It's a stupid idea and –

Mahak licks me.

He uses his tongue on my most intimate, private spot, breathing in my scent, blowing on my wetness. I feel his stubble on my inner thighs and open my legs wider.

I forget about ever wanting him to stop.

Mahak opens me with his thumbs, using his tongue to explore me, slowly and carefully. Again and again, his tongue travels the length of me, back and forth until my entire being is focused on the small area with the countless nerve endings, my most secret area. I can't think of why it needs to be so private. This should be shared, enjoyed.

Mahak tongues my nub and I cry out in shock. Then he plunges his tongue inside me.

Nathan has touched me with his fingers many, many times. But I have never allowed him to have this intimacy. Even though he's my husband and I love him, I've never felt comfortable enough to let him use his mouth...there. But Mahak never gave me a choice so there's nothing I can do.

He licks me slowly, the crux of my private part, circling it slowly, then faster. The added wetness of his tongue, the heat from his mouth, the feel of his firm tongue against the delicate skin have brought about sensations I never knew existed. My entire being is centred between my legs. Mahak tucks his hands under my bum and pulls me closer, angling me for better access. He lashes with his tongue and the sound of the wetness mixes with my little whimpering cries in the room.

And then he surrounds it with his mouth and sucks on it.

"Oh, my God," I cry out.

Mahak lifts his head and smiles wolfishly at me. "Do you still want me to stop?"

"No, oh God no!" I strain against my bindings, shamelessly arching towards him, desperate for his touch again.

"What do you want me to do? Tell me."

"No, please, just keep doing that."

"Tell me," he demands. "I want to hear you say it. Tell me or I'll stop." He leans over my pussy and licks me full with his tongue, finishing at my clit and then he lifts his head again. "What do you want me to do?"

"Your tongue," I stammer. "Please! Use your mouth."

"You like it?"

"Yes! Please, please, don't stop."

I hear him chuckle and then I don't hear anything as he resumes his attack with his tongue.

His tongue, his fingers explore every inch of me. I unashamedly spread my legs, wanting Mahak to have access to my private parts, my secret spots only Nathan had seen and touched. I want Mahak to plunder me, every part of me.

And he does. He licks every inch of me and I'm so consumed with these new sensations that I don't shy away when I feel his tongue probing an even more intimate spot. He licks me front to back, back and forth, slow at first, taking time to plunge his tongue inside me before replacing it with his fingers, thrusting them in and out while he licks me.

I've had three orgasms so I know what I'm feeling, but it's never been like this. I don't even realize how much noise I'm making – moaning and whimpering and wordlessly crying out. All I can concentrate on is the sensation of Mahak's mouth on me. And then there's a build-up in my core and I begin pushing myself brazenly against his mouth, desperate for Mahak to continue, to take every inch of me.

It's too much. I can't bear this. All the sensations, his mouth against me, his tongue—

And then I explode.

I scream, pushing myself up, arching my back, still unable to use my hands to push down on his head like I want to.

But Mahak doesn't stop. He keeps using his tongue on me, slowing momentarily while I catch my breath, and then faster again, not giving me time to recover.

I don't want to recover. I don't want him to stop. I want more.

Mahak focuses on my little nub with his tongue, twirling, circling, lashing. His fingers thrust inside me, hard and fast. He finds a spot inside me that makes me cry out again.

I writhe on the bed, pulling at the restraints, pushing my hips up against his mouth. I've never felt this out of control before.

"Don't stop," I beg. "Oh, god, please don't stop."

And then I spiral completely out of control.

The second time is even more intense. I feel like I'm flying, spinning out of control as the orgasm hits me again and again, and I can't bear it any longer.

Finally, Mahak slows, giving me one last lick before he lifts his head, giving me his wolfish smile.

"Did you like that?"

I can only smile weakly and he doesn't give me a chance to respond, before he's on me, pulling my legs up and out of the way as he moves between them. I have a frisson of fear remembering how big he is; *this is going to hurt*. I catch my breath as he pushes inside me, slowly but without any gentleness.

I have one last conscious thought, *I can't believe I'm doing this* before Mahak starts to move. I can't move even if I want to, with my arms held and his weight holding me down.

"I knew you'd like it," Mahak says as he slowly moves within me. "Next time will be even better."

I think I might want a next time.

Mahak thrusts into me, steadily and I'm moving my hips to his rhythm, wanting more. And then he stops, rearing up and brushing the hair out of my eyes.

"Am I hurting you?" he asks with sweet concern. "You are so tiny."

"No," I whimper. He isn't but his weight between my legs isn't exactly pleasant.

"Try this." Mahak pulls out and quickly unties me and I automatically rub away the numbness of my wrists. Then he lays on the bed beside me, helping me to climb astride him. With his hands on my hips to guide me, he helps me slide onto him.

I gasp at the sensation.

"Is that better? Don't move," he instructs. He grasps my waist with both hands and thrusts up.

I gasp again, feeling him push inside me. I shift my weight, using my muscles to lift off him, then down. Up and down. I move a little quicker. Up and down.

"Don't move," Mahak orders. "Stay completely still."

I'm not sure that's possible.

But he thrusts up again, lifting me up slightly, before lowering me. Same movement I was doing, but once again, I've lost the control.

I place my hands on his chest and close my eyes and let myself enjoy the sensation of being impaled by his cock.

Mahak starts out slowly, rhythmically, filling me completely with every thrust. Then he speeds up, and I'm making little whimpering noises, wanting more. I want him hard and fast, but I'm not there –I can't tell him that. I've lost some of the utter abandonment I felt when he was tonguing me. My body is responding to Mahak, but I'm conscious of what I'm doing once more.

And then Mahak moves his hand so his thumb is against me and I cry out involuntarily at the added sensation.

With the pressure of his hands removed from my waist, I immediately start to ride him, pressing my hands against his chest for support. Up and down, up and down, sometimes rising so high only his tip is within me, before falling back on him. Hard and as fast as I can, taking control, only allowing Mahak to use his fingers against me.

My legs are burning but I can't stop. I'm making strange, harsh cries I've never heard before. I want more, more of his *cock* inside me, more of his fingers playing me, more –

And then I come, bucking wildly astride him, with my head thrown back. My cry becomes a scream as my body takes over once more, convulsing joyously.

Mahak's hands again grip my waist tightly as he thrusts upwards, his face contorted in an expression of pleasure. He is smiling at me as he comes and I can't help but laugh as I slow my movements.

"I told you I'd make you scream," he says.

"When *can* we do that again?" I ask with delight, proud of myself.

I can't wait to get home to my husband.

Jackson

WENDY MADE ME WORK from home today to deal with the pool guys.

Yes, it was my idea to put in a pool, but I thought she was on board with it. But now, it's like she expects me to deal with everything about it, including talking to the workers because we don't like how they've finished the tile. She says the men don't respect her and won't listen to her. I told her to use her 'mom' voice she uses with the kids and any guy will instantly know she's one tough-ass chick. She didn't like that suggestion.

Which is why I'm working from home today.

Trying to work from home. Unfortunately, I'm not doing a very good job. Between an afternoon Jays baseball game on television and the new Halo game I haven't had time to master, I know I'm not going to be very productive. And Wendy was at Melissa's this morning and took the kids to some reading thing at the library so it's not like she's around to crack the whip.

Wendy cracking a whip. Nice image, although unrealistic.

Wendy has been open to a lot more things lately, thanks to the arrangement with the neighbours. Actually, it's more than the key parties. That took a little persuading at the beginning, but I had help from Molly and Melissa. Not that I did much. When we got the invitation from Tia, I wasn't sure how to handle things. Yes, I would love to be able to have sex with the ladies on the street without worrying about divorce court or a sharp stick to the privates, but I couldn't tell *Wendy* that. It had to be her decision. It had to be her suggestion, actually.

And that's where Melissa and Molly came in. They convinced Wendy and then Paige and we've been one happy, polyamorous neighbourhood since then.

Polyamory. I looked the word up. It means we're swingers.

I miss Molly and Jason. She was a real, little spitfire and Jason was a cool guy to hang out with when I wasn't having sex with his wife. I think Wendy might have had more than a little crush on Jason, but I couldn't figure out how to ask her about it. But then all of a sudden they moved and then Jacey and Dominic bought the house and took their spot at the parties.

Jacey reminds me of Molly sometimes. I like a woman who likes sex as much as she does.

I wonder if Jacey would be into something like whips? I bet Tia would be. *That* would be a turn-on, scary but sexier than hell. Tia's always done it for me.

I don't get enough time with that lady.

I've known Tia for years and I feel like I don't know anything about her. Wendy is close to her and I can hold my own in a conversation, but I have no idea what makes her tick. Like, how did she come up with the idea to have a key party at her house once a month, and invite the neighbours? Not that I'm complaining – the woman made me a swinger and my sex life is pretty damn good because of it. It was good before we started mixing and matching, but Wendy and I have been together since high school and that's a long time. Everyone needs a little excitement and variety helps out with that. Besides, Wendy and I always have the best sex after one of Tia's little get-togethers!

I've almost decided the day is a total write-off when the door rings. Wendy pulled out only a few minutes ago, so I think it's her, forgetting something and not wanting to turn off the car. So I pull open the door with a big smile and find Melissa standing there.

"Hey?" I say with confusion.

Melissa is like Tia – I've known her for years, I've done some nasty stuff with her, but I don't really feel like I *know* her. I've lived three doors down from her and Mahak for four years and I don't think I've ever been alone in the house with her.

I can't help but picture Melissa with a whip.

"Wendy asked to borrow a book from me," Melissa says, smacking a paperback with the palm of her hand which somehow only increases my image of her as a dominatrix. Black leather catsuit and sky-high heels? Mmm... "I thought I'd bring it over."

Without waiting for an invite or even for me to move out of the way, Melissa brushes past me into the house and steps out of her flip-flops before heading into the living room.

"Wendy's not here right now," I tell her, shutting the door after her.

"I know," Melissa calls from the other room. "Oh, Blue Jays game!"

"You like baseball?" I ask, truly dumbfounded.

"Of course! I grew up playing it," Melissa says. "But Mahak's not really into it so I hardly ever watch it these days. He only likes tennis and cricket."

"I don't understand cricket," I confess.

"Me neither." The two of us stand in front of the wall-mounted, HD television that I'm inordinately proud of, even though it's not quite as large as Mahak's.

That's the story about everything on this street.

Bautista is up to bat with a 2-2 count. As we watch, he swings at a sliding fastball for a third strike.

"He's over-rated as a player," Melissa comments as Bautista, the Jays greatest hope for post-season play, walks back to the dugout.

"It was a strike-out. He's .289 with a .306 slugging average," I argue.

"This is the guy I like," she ignores me as Edwin Encarnacion steps up to bat. "Watch. Out of the park." Wouldn't you know it, on the second pitch, Encarnacion takes a mighty swing to send it flying over the fence. "What did I tell you?"

"You were just lucky. He was due." I glance curiously at Melissa, transfixed by the game. "Hey, uh, so do you want to watch with me for a while?"

"I thought you were supposed to be working? That's what your wife said." She glances warily at me and I'm struck by how cute she is, with her short, blonde hair and big eyes. She's got a wicked body, too, as I've seen for myself many times.

Unfortunately, Melissa can be irritating a lot of the time, so you forget about her cute face and awesome body. Today, finding out abot she likes baseball, helps me forget how annoying she can be.

"Well, Wen's not here right now, is she?" I grin. "Sit down. Want something to drink? Coffee, maybe? There's still some in the pot."

"What about a beer?" she muses, following me into the kitchen. "Seems only right if we're watching the game."

"Beer. Great idea," I say, and head out to the garage where the second fridge is stocked with beer and pop and other things that aren't considered child-friendly. "You're just full of surprises today," I tell her as I hand her an icy bottle.

"You have no idea," she grins at me.

We're back in the living room, settled in our seats, in time to watch the third out. During the commercial, we talk baseball and I'm amazed to discover Melissa is quite knowledgeable about the sport.

"I had no idea," I marvel.

"What, that I was interested in anything more than sex?"

"You do seem to enjoy sex quite a bit," I say carefully.

"And you don't?" she counters.

"Well," I hesitate, and she laughs.

We move on to kids and then she dutifully asks me about work. Before long, three innings have passed and we're on our second beer.

"This is nice," Melissa says, raising her bottle to me. Maybe I should have offered her a glass.

"It is. Once it stopped being a little weird," I confess.

"It was strange," she agrees. "Why can't husbands and wives hang out?"

"Husbands and wives of other people? Because we're usually too busy having sex."

"True," she nods. "We do that a lot."

"I always thought it wasn't enough."

"And you think *I'm* too interested in sex?" she protests.

"I never said it was too much!"

I'm sitting in my living room, watching the Jays game and drinking a beer. With Melissa. And I'm having a good time with her. *With our clothes on!*

It boggles the mind.

"So what book did Wen want to borrow?" I ask to fill the sudden silence.

Melissa holds up the book she still has in her hand. "*Diary of a Submissive.*"

"*Really*? You're kidding! Wendy's not into that."

"Don't you know what your wife reads?"

"I know she reads romance books with heaving bosoms and sexy cowboys, and she's run through those Fifty Shades stuff, but I didn't think she was into submissive stuff."

Melissa shrugs. "I'm not into it either. I think I'd be the more dominant type."

"I was thinking the same thing."

"Not that I've tried it," she continues as if I haven't spoken. "Mahak would never be into it."

"Being spanked and tied up and all that? No, can't see him being much into that!"

"You'd be surprised," she smirks. "I tell him what to do all the time and he doesn't seem to mind that."

"Thank you for the image of your husband in ass-less chaps and a dog collar. Really appreciate it."

Melissa laughs and I can't help but notice she has a great laugh. "I'd pay money to see that."

"Maybe he can dress up for Halloween," I suggest.

"Never in public." She tosses the book on the coffee table beside her and takes a drink of her beer. "It wasn't a bad book. It goes into paddling and pain but it's kind of gross how descriptive it is."

"Like how? The sex scenes?"

"I don't mind those, but I really don't want to know how wet a girl is, how stuff is dripping down her legs."

"Maybe not that descriptive," I agree, furiously attempting to stop thinking about Melissa's pussy, all tight and snug under those yoga pants. I shift in the chair, replacing the image of Melissa with a whip, which doesn't help the erection which is making a tent-like structure in my shorts.

"Other than that, it's pretty good," Melissa continues, oblivious to the effect she's having on me. "A few sexy scenes."

"Is that what you like?" I ask carefully. "Do you like reading books like that?"

"Sure. But we're kind of living it, don't you think?"

"You mean with everything going on at Tia's?" This is more than strange. I've never talked to anyone about what we're involved in and never thought it would be Melissa who I had the first conversation with.

Melissa shrugs again. "And outside Tia's. I think people are beginning to play during off-hours."

"Really?" It's embarrassing the way my voice cracks. "Are you guys?"

"Mahak has something going on with Jacey in the mornings," she says nonchalantly. "And didn't Wendy tell you what went on at my place that day?"

"No..."

This time she smiles at me. "I'll let her tell you. I'll just say I saw a new side of your wife that day."

I frantically try to think of a reason Melissa would say that, something that isn't sex-related.

I can't come up with anything.

I'm not sure what the expression on my face is but when I look over at her, Melissa is looking at me and laughing. "What you're thinking is probably right."

"Wendy?" I burst out. "But she..."

"...is becoming much more adventurous. You should be happy."

"I am. But the two of you just decided one morning...?"

"No, it was the four of us. I thought we needed to be more comfortable together, which would open us up for more experiences. It was fun."

"Fun...Is this a usual thing?"

"We only did it once. But then I decided I needed to get practice at giving blow jobs and invited Joe over."

"You – really? Joe, with the four of you? Wendy never said anything about *that*."

"No, it was just Joe. And Jacey. I think there's something going on with the two of them."

"You and Joe and Jacey. Because you wanted to learn how to give a blow-job?"

"That's right."

"You can always practice on me," I tell her weakly.

"Well, that's partly the reason I stopped by," Melissa astounds me by saying. "The book was just an excuse."

And then she's standing before me, fingering the hem of her shirt. Melissa is fairly short, and the armchair I'm sitting in is a big one, so I'm at eye level with her breasts.

Melissa has very nice breasts. I know she's had work done to them because I've had first-hand knowledge of them, but it doesn't make them any less nice.

I wrench my eyes away from her chest and look up at her. Melissa is smiling at me, a cocky, smug little smile. "It's been a while, hasn't it?"

"It has." I'm clutching my beer in my hand and put it on the table carefully. I have an urge to reach out and grab Melissa and have an inkling I'm going to be able to do just that so I want to have both hands free. But I wait patiently to see what's going to happen.

"Does Wendy ever tell you what to do?" Melissa asks me.

I shake my head and force myself to look her in the eyes again. "Not really."

"I think I'd like to try that," Melissa muses. "But we both know Mahak wouldn't go for it."

"You're probably right."

Melissa nods and continues looking down at me, head cocked to the side like she's appraising me. Then she pulls her T-shirt over her head. Her bra is pink with lace, which I never would have expected and full to overflowing with those luscious tits.

So much for having fun while fully dressed.

Instinctively I reach out to her with both hands.

"Did I say you could touch?" she asks in a cold voice.

"No, but...you're standing right there and you look so good."

"I know I look good but I never said you could touch." Melissa bends at the waist and pulls down her pants, along with her underwear. Then she unhooks her bra, leaving everything pooled on the floor at her feet. "Do you have a problem with this?"

"Uh, *no.*"

"With me telling you what to do?"

I lean back in my chair with my arms tucked behind my head. "Whatever you want."

I've always liked Melissa and we've always had fun together, but it's always been average everyday sex. Vanilla sex, I think it's called. There's nothing wrong with that, and I heartily enjoy sex of any flavour, but I suspect today is going to be a little different.

I think I'm up for it.

At least part of me is.

Melissa moves closer and kneels on the chair, her knees touching my thighs as she straddles me. "Don't touch until I tell you to." She leans over me, cradling her breasts in her hands until her tight nipples are level with my mouth. "Tongue them. And then suck. No hands."

I can do nothing but obey. Resistance is futile.

I eagerly lap at her nipples, so firm and erect, one at a time before returning to suck forcefully on them. This goes on for several minutes and I'm proud of my willpower not to reach out my hands and pull Melissa down onto my lap and grind her against my hard cock now straining against my shorts.

Melissa finally leans back, leaving me reaching out with my tongue. "I want you to lick my pussy," she orders coolly. "Until I come. And if you don't do a good enough job, I'm not going to touch you. I'm not going to put your big, hard dick in my mouth and suck it until you're dry. Ok?"

"I, I'll do my best," I stammer. Talk about pressure!

I let Melissa to decide on the position. Being quite athletic and obviously flexible, she climbs up on the arms of the chair, balancing on her knees so her pussy is almost level with my mouth. "You can use your hands now," she commands.

I don't have to be told twice. I grab her tight, little ass and pull it towards me, scrunching down in the chair to make it easier. Then I press my mouth against her pussy, so smooth and shaven. I probe between her lips with my tongue, hearing her quick intake of breath as I touch her clit. Without waiting for her next instructions, I push my face forward and begin to lap her with fast, firm strokes of my tongue.

I'm not Mahak. I haven't perfected the art of oral sex like he has, but I do my best. The thought of Melissa's mouth on me is a great inspiration. I snake my hand around her ass and push a finger into her pussy, feeling the warm wetness as it slides inside.

"I like that," Melissa says breathlessly as I begin circling her clit with my tongue. "Hard, and fast, just like that."

I continue, per her request, per her command. Is this what she wants? To tell me what to do?

I'm fine with that. I'm always in charge in the bedroom with Wendy and with everyone else, so it's a nice change to sit back and be told what to do, and when to do it...I think.

Melissa begins to make little cries that grow louder as I increase the pressure on her pussy. This isn't the best position to be in, but I do my best, thrusting my fingers in and out of her in rhythm to her hips pushing against me.

"Wait, wait," she gasps suddenly. "I need more." But then she climbs off the chair. "Get on the floor," she instructs. "Hurry."

I scramble to the floor, lying prone as she orders. As soon as I'm in position, she straddles me, facing my feet. "Keep going," she says, pressing her pussy against my waiting mouth. I grip her hips and begin to move her so she's rocking back and forth against my tongue, the sounds of her wetness and her moans mixing in the room.

From a distance, I can hear the excited voice of the commentary and resist the urge to see what's going on in the game. Melissa would not appreciate that.

I'm really glad I didn't because Melissa's hands are suddenly at my waist, undoing the buttons of my shorts. I instantly let go of her hips and help her; together we manage to get them pushed down enough so my cock is released. And then Melissa bends so that she can take it in her mouth.

I don't remember the last time I had a 69.

I groan as soon as she takes me in her mouth because it feels so very good. I'm playing with Melissa's clit at the time with my lips and tongue and it must give her an added vibration because she cries out, the noise muffled by my cock filling her mouth. She's running her mouth along the length of me, with little flickers of her tongue around the head. I can feel the occasional bite of her teeth as well, which only adds to the sensation.

From the feel of it, Melissa has been practicing a whole lot.

It's hard to concentrate now, but I do my best, licking and sucking her clit, using my tongue to explore her folds. Melissa is moving her hips, grinding her pussy against me. I focus on her clit, using my tongue like a finger, frantically swirling it around the nub. Just as I take it in my mouth and suck it, Melissa gives a high-pitched cry, her hips convulsing under my hands as she comes.

For a brief second, I worry about my cock, but then I relax and enjoy the sensation of a woman reaching orgasm with me in her mouth.

After her body stills, Melissa rears up. "That was pretty good," she says breathlessly.

"Gee, thanks but—"

"I need you to fuck me now," she continues. "Hard and fast. Now."

Who am I to argue? Even though the blow job was feeling pretty damn good.

Melissa climbs off me and gets on all fours. "There's a condom in my pants," she instructs.

'In her pants' means a tiny, hidden pocket in her waistband. It takes me a minute to find it.

I get on my knees behind her and slide my cock into her waiting, wet pussy. She drops her head to the floor.

"It's not going to take me long," I confess as I give a mighty thrust.

"Oh, come on, Jackson, you have more willpower than that. I want you to make me come again. Make me scream."

"I can make you scream," I tell her, pulling my cock out slowly until I've got just the tip at the opening of her pussy. Then I slam into her.

"Just like that," Melissa cries. "Fuck me like that."

"I'll fuck you anyway I want to," I decide. Enough of this bullshit of being told what to do. "I'm in charge now."

"Oh, God," she moans, making no argument.

"You like it?" I ask. "You like my dick fucking you?" When she doesn't respond I reach and grab the back of her hair. "Do you?" I thrust hard against her.

"Yes!" she cries, her voice and the way she's pushing back against me, tells me exactly how much she likes it.

"Use your hand," I order her. Willpower or not, the memory of her mouth on me has guaranteed that this will be quick. I don't want to leave her unsatisfied.

I'm afraid to.

Melissa uses her hand between her legs and I let go of her hair to grab her hips. I pull her back onto me with every thrust; drawing back as far as I can before slamming forward. "Your pussy feels so good," I groan.

"Go faster," she begs.

I comply, only because I want to. I know I'm going to come in a minute. I fuck Melissa as fast and as hard as I can and soon the two of us are rocking along the floor, Melissa frantically using her fingers, both of us making enough noise to be heard outside.

Melissa cries out again, her back arching under my onslaught, her pussy tightening around my cock as she comes. That's all it takes for me.

"Fuck me," I shout and with a final, massive thrust that pushes Melissa along the rug, I empty into her.

Neither of us can say anything as I pull out of her, both breathing hard. Melissa reaches for her pants and I hand her the T-shirt before standing up and pulling on my shorts.

"You don't take orders very well," Melissa finally says.

"I think there's a limit," I grin and she smiles in return. "Your blowjob technique is pretty good."

"I've never had any complaints," she brags.

"But you never give blowjobs," I point out. "At least not for me."

Is that pink I see on Melissa's cheeks? "I'm getting used to it," she admits quietly. We dress in silence, which quickly becomes awkward.

"I guess I'll go now," Melissa says.

I glance at the television where the game is still on. "4-1 for the Jays," I tell her. "Want to finish your beer and watch a little more?"

So she does.

Mahak

MY WIFE CAN BE trying at times.

I adore her with all my heart but sometimes she can be a bit much. She's demanding, has no qualms about speaking her mind, often about things she doesn't have the knowledge to have an opinion about and needs to be the centre of attention at all times. Plus, recently, she's begun to think she's an expert on all things related to sex. She even had the audacity to critique my performance the other night!

I've been with other women. I've heard no complaints.

The memory of Jacey from last week is still fresh in my mind; her taste and touch and the sounds she made when she reached orgasm. I made her come with my tongue and fingers in only a few minutes while we were in the front seat of my car. Not everyone can say that. And what I did for sweet Emma at Tia's Saturday night—she was trembling with fright when I first touched her.

Of course, I made her tremble in a different way by the end of it.

But there are times when Melissa surprises me and I recall why it was such a good idea to marry her.

Like tonight.

I had to work late, which isn't unusual, and Melissa had made plans, which is. She told me she had gotten in touch with an old friend via Facebook a few weeks ago and the two had made plans to go out that night for dinner. Amid many grumblings that I wasn't capable of being home with the kids that night on my own, Melissa made arrangements for the kids to sleep over at her parents. I was expecting to come home after work to an unusually empty and blessedly quiet house.

I'm still a little irritated at Melissa's criticisms the other night. Perhaps I should mention that if she doesn't appreciate what I do to help her reach orgasm, she is welcome to find other ways to do it, such as doing it herself.

For some reason, Melissa doesn't like to masturbate. On occasion, she's helped herself along, but she'd rather have someone else do it.

I had no problem with it. In fact, that's what I'm planning on doing in my quiet and empty house when I get home.

I can't help but speculate if Melissa is going elsewhere for her enjoyment.

We have been enjoying the company of our neighbours for some time now. The gatherings at Tia's allow us to experience each other in ways most neighbours don't get to experience each other. Each of us had gained knowledge and skills with the opposite sex that can only benefit our marriages. I think the evenings have helped all the wives become much more adventurous. I was amazed when Melissa told me about helping Wendy and Paige overcome their aversions to being with a woman. I look forward to seeing how Melissa's teachings have helped them.

I'm not sure if Melissa knows about my arrangement with Jacey. Not that we have an arrangement, per se. Jacey and I enjoy each other and have taken to meeting occasionally before I head off to work. Jacey likes oral sex and I'm quite good at giving it, regardless of what my wife might think. And Jacey has no misgivings about returning the favour. Dominic is a lucky man.

If Melissa has a problem with my interludes with Jacey, it might be that she is jealous. I think she's quite taken with Jacey. Her suggestion to invite Jacey for an afternoon of play in our bedroom surprised me. Melissa had previously been with Tia but hadn't ever expressed any interest in being with another woman.

First Jacey, and then Valentine's Day. I was proud of my little Melissa that night. That night, she proved to me and everyone at the party that she was ready for anything.

I'm thinking of the afternoon with Jacey and Melissa as I pull into the driveway, so caught up in my thoughts, that I don't notice Melissa's car is beside me in the garage until I get out. Another car is parked on the street outside the house.

Looks like there will be no solo satisfaction for me that evening.

"Mahak?" Melissa calls as soon she hears the door open. Most nights she comes and meets me at the door, usually with a child in tow, but always with a hello kiss. Tonight, she only calls out to me.

"You're home early," I reply, slipping off my shoes.

"We're in the family room. Come have some wine."

We? Maybe Jacey has stopped by. Maybe it would be an interesting evening after all.

But it isn't Jacey with Melissa.

Instead, a curvy woman with a pretty face and masses of blonde curly hair sits on the couch beside Melissa.

She has the most amazing breasts.

I am a breast man.

I love all aspects of a woman's body but I find myself lost in thrall when faced with a truly spectacular pair of breasts. And whoever she is, this woman has a pair I'm instantly fixated on.

"This is Evie," Melissa says proudly. "I convinced her to come and meet you."

"But I wasn't home," I say with rare confusion, transfixed by the sight of this strange and attractive woman on the couch drinking wine with Melissa.

It's odd to see Melissa drink more than a glass of wine. There is a half-empty bottle on the coffee table in front of them.

"We thought we could find something to amuse us while we wait," Melissa giggles.

The wine must have gone to her head. My wife never giggles. She looks nice, for once not wearing her standard yoga pants. She always fills out the pants nicely, but it's a treat to see her wearing something else for once.

"It's nice to meet you, Mahak," Evie says, standing up and moving towards me. I stand stock still as she throws her arms around me in a tight hug, her breasts pressing against my chest. She kisses my cheek, before pulling away. "You were right," Evie turns back to Melissa. "He *is* hot."

"Yes, he is," Melissa says proudly, still on the couch. "And he's all *mine*."

"You're lucky," Evie says wistfully, still standing close to me, her hand on my arm. I can smell her perfume, some flirty, flowery fragrance and still feel the weight of her breasts against my chest. What is going on here? Have they both drunk too much and is this some sort of female pissing contest?

"I like to share," Melissa continues, the suggestion in her voice crystal clear.

"Do you like to be shared?" Evie asks me, her eyes wide, looking a little shyly at me.

I glance from Evie to Melissa. "What exactly is going on here?" I ask. I'm not sure if this is some game they are playing, or if they're serious about what I think they are implying.

If they're serious, I'm all for it. If not, I don't want to be involved in a silly game.

"I brought my wonderful husband a present," Melissa tells me. "I thought you might enjoy an evening with Evie as much as I did." She pulls herself off the couch and comes to Evie's side. "As much as I will."

She leans forward and kisses Evie then, touching her breast with her hand. Evie splays her hand against my chest and as Melissa pulls away, Evie clutches my shirt and pulls me forward to kiss her.

I've been with two women before but never before have they been this forward. Not even Tia.

"I'll go get you a glass of wine," Melissa tells me as Evie is exploring my mouth with her tongue and my fingers itch to touch those breasts. "You'll need something to cool you off when you watch us."

I sense Melissa moving away; as soon as she does, Evie takes my hand and presses it onto her breast. "I know you want to," she whispers into my mouth. "You can't stop looking at them. Do you know how much that turns me on?"

I cup Evie's full breasts with both hands as she slides a hand down to feel my cock, hard and confined. She rubs her hand along my length and I can't help but shove forward. She laughs deep in her throat.

"You're a bad boy, aren't you?" she says huskily, her lips barely grazing mine now. She darts out her tongue and licks my top lip. I can taste the wine on her breath. "Such a big, *bad* boy. I can't wait until I have your cock inside me." She gives my cock a final squeeze and backs away, my hands still reaching for her. "But first I'm going to fuck your wife. While you watch."

Melissa is back and she hands me a glass of wine. "Why don't you have a seat?" she asks me politely.

"I don't...what...?" I'm embarrassed to admit how befuddled I am. I feel like I've walked into a dream. Or a fantasy. I've never had a woman like Evie. She's so forceful, aggressive, almost like a man. The way she kissed me, touched me, almost as if she has every right to use me like she wants to.

I think I like it.

I take the glass from Melissa and sit in the centre chair, the one directly in front of the television. Without waiting for me to be settled, Melissa joins Evie in front of me and they begin touching each other.

"You've never just watched, have you?" Evie asks me, her hands full of Melissa's breasts, her lips against the soft skin of my wife's neck. "Does it turn you on?"

I can only nod my consent, unable to tear my eyes away from her hands on Melissa.

"Please answer when I ask you a question," Evie says sharply, surprising me. "Does it turn you on?"

"Yes," I reply in a low voice.

"What do you want me to do to her?" Evie asks. "Anything you want."

"Take her clothes off."

Without hesitation, Evie begins unbuttoning Melissa's blouse, working each button slowly with her fingers, Melissa's hands hanging by her side. Between every button, Evie kisses her, and I watch their lips press together, the brief sight of tongues making me even harder. Soon the blouse hangs open but before Evie removes it, she cups Melissa's breasts in her hands, trailing her tongue along the lace of her bra. Melissa's eyes are closed and she brings a hand up to the back of Evie's head. Evie pushes the sheer fabric of Melissa's blouse off her shoulders onto the floor and reaches around to unclasp Melissa's bra. Soon it falls to the floor as well, and Evie strokes Melissa's breast, using her fingers to surround the nipple, pulling it into a point. She bends her head to the other side, and I watch as her tongue darts out to lick Melissa's nipple.

Melissa's intake of breath is loud in the silent room.

I think I might be in heaven.

"Did you want me to touch her like this?" Evie says, laying her head on Melissa's breast and looking at me. "Do you like watching me touch her like this?"

"Yes," I say hoarsely.

"Do you think she likes it?"

"Yes."

Evie switches sides then, and I can see by Melissa's posture how she is enjoying this. Her breath is coming in little gasps, both hands pressed against Evie's blonde head.

The front of my pants feels uncomfortably tight.

After a few minutes of this magnificent view and listening to Melissa making little moaning noise, Evie raises her head again and looks at me with a smug smile. "I'm going to take off her pants now. Would you like that?"

"Yes," I mutter, thinking I'd like to rip them off and plunge into her; first Melissa and then that aggravating Evie. The woman knows exactly what this is doing to me and is clearly enjoying it!

"Why don't you take yours off as well?" Evie suggests as she slowly works the button on Melissa's black pants, and then the zipper, slowly pulling it up and down to torment me. "Please take your pants off."

"Is that an order?" I growl.

Evie shrugs, still with a smug smile on her face. "No orders. Merely a request for you to be more... comfortable. While I make your wife feel even more comfortable."

She's not going to continue unless I undress. Evie's point is clear. With a grimace and frustrated fingers, I pull off my pants. "Everything," Evie says, raising her eyebrows with admiration.

She doesn't take off Melissa's pants until I'm naked and seated back in the chair. The leather is uncomfortable against my bare skin.

Once I'm undressed, the rest of Melissa's clothes come off in quick succession, leaving Evie the only one fully dressed. I've never been with a woman who has taken charge so completely. She refuses to let Melissa do anything to assist and barely lets her touch her.

"Why don't you take off your clothes too?" I ask as Evie settles Melissa on the floor before me.

"Why don't I?" she says lightly and begins to undress. "You'd like to see that, wouldn't you? To see exactly what you're going to be fucking soon?"

"Yes."

Evie smiles as she takes off her clothes, leaving those full and awe-inspiring breasts free and unfettered. She's curvy and rounded, with belly and thighs that make petite Melissa look like a child, but in my eyes, I've never seen anyone so sexy and wanton. I can't wait to fuck her. I want to stick my dick between those beautiful breasts, and then her pussy...

"I like to be fucked slowly at first," Evie tells me once her clothes in a heap on the floor. "And then when I'm begging for it – and I will beg for it – really hard and fast. Could you do that?"

"I can," I tell her, confidently while inside I'm almost panting in excitement.

"But I want your wife first," Evie reminds me. She leans over Melissa and drops a kiss on her stomach, then tells her. "I'll be right back."

"What?" Melissa gasps, raising herself up on her elbows to watch Evie pull something out of her purse.

"Forgot my little friends," Evie smiles at her, taking out a smooth, purple vibrator and a larger white one from a little cloth bag. "One for me, too."

I can only watch as she kneels on the floor beside Melissa – on the other side so I can watch – and runs her hands across Melissa's breasts and down her stomach. "You have a beautiful body," she tells her. "And so do you," she adds, looking up at me. "Why don't you touch yourself?"

The way her fingers hover over Melissa's thighs suggests once again she's waiting for me to comply. I grasp my cock with my hand and her smile widens.

"Do you know how much of a turn-on that is?" she says in a low voice, spreading Melissa's legs open with a hand and holding one of the vibrators with the other. "I love to see a man with enough balls to pleasure himself in front of a woman. Does that turn you on, too? Watching Melissa touch herself? If I were to touch myself?"

I nod as I slide my hand along my shaft. Apparently, that's enough of a response, because Evie flips the vibrator on and touches it between Melissa's legs. Melissa gasps and opens her legs wider and I see her pussy, pink and wet. Evie uses the vibrator to stroke her like a lazy finger, circling her clit with the buzzing tip before thrusting it inside her.

"Like that?" Evie asks Melissa.

"Uh huh," Melissa gasps, arching her back so her hips press upward.

I like that too, I think to myself.

Evie smiles as she thrusts it inside her and then returns it to her clit.

"It's fun that we can all play together," Evie says conversationally. With one hand, she plays with Melissa and with the other she reaches for the other vibrator. With a flip of her thumb, a second buzzing sound fills the room. Evie rises up on her knees and slips it between her own legs. "Ah, that does feel nice."

I watch, dry-mouthed, as Evie uses the one vibrator on Melissa and the other on herself. My hand grasps my cock tightly and almost on its own accord, strokes the length of the shaft, slowly at first, then faster. I watch the purple plastic dip and dart through Melissa's pussy. Her eyes are closed, and she's making little cries now, thrusting her hips into the air shamelessly. Evie never takes her eyes off me as she pleasures herself with the sex toy.

I don't know if I've ever seen anything so exciting, live, right in front of me. Some of the scenes at Tia's have come close, but there's been nothing like this. No one has been as wanton as Evie.

"I'm going to come soon," Evie announces. Melissa is making so much noise that I doubt she can hear her, but I suspect she's close to orgasm as well. "I want to watch you come as well."

"But –" I protest. I'm not about to stop or even move my hand away but I do want to fuck her. I want to fuck her so hard it hurts.

"Later," she whispers. "I'm not going anywhere."

I close my eyes briefly, only to have them flash open as Evie gives a long, drawn-out moan. "Are you almost ready?" she asks.

I begin to frantically pull on my cock. "Almost. Melissa..."

"Any second." And before she can finish, Melissa releases a series of high-pitched cries that signify her orgasm. Evie continues with the vibrator and Melissa keeps thrusting upwards.

"Now," Evie gasps and she throws her head back with a sharp cry, shivering as the sensations raced through her body.

With a growl-like groan, I come into my own hand.

Everything goes blank for a moment until I realize the room has quieted.

"That was fun, wasn't it?" Evie says brightly, jumping to her feet, her rosy cheeks the only indication of what just happened.

That, and the two vibrators in her hand.

"I'll get something to clean you up," she says, heading into the kitchen. I watch her go, enjoying the sight of her bare ass.

"How did you say you know her?" I ask Melissa in a low voice.

Melissa smiles sheepishly at me. "I really don't. Do you remember Serena from the Valentine's party? Where we...?"

"I remember. The image of you on that pool table is etched in my mind forever," I smile at my adventurous little wife.

"Well, she's been in touch with me. We've talked...about different things...and she suggested I give Evie a call. Said it might be fun for us."

"So she's not your friend?" I ask as Evie returns with a roll of paper towels. She smiles as she unwinds some from the roll.

"No," Evie answers before Melissa does. "But I would like to become both of your... friends?" She gives me a suggestive smile and my eyes fall on those breasts and I think of what I'd like to do to her.

"We could try that," Melissa says, giving me a sly look. "I think we'd be good friends."

I love my wife.

"But not tonight," Evie tells us. "Not tonight. I'm going to get out of here and leave the two of you alone to fuck like rabbits. But call me. Soon."

We don't even wait to see Evie drive away before I'm racing Melissa to our bedroom.

Next up from our naughty neighbours? Interludes II!

Interludes II

ANNA ELLIS

THREE BIRDS PRESS

Contents

Wendy

"I BLAME COLIN FOR the pool," I say as I sink into the churning waters of the hot tub.

"Don't you mean to give him credit?" Jacey asks from where she is sitting across from me, holding a glass of wine above the bubbles and looking very cozy with my husband, Jackson.

"You didn't want a pool?" Dominic asks, handing me back my wine glass. I had gone in to check on the kids to find all of them still asleep. We had invited Jacey and Dominic over with their kids, Hanna and Ben, for dinner and somehow the four of us ended up in our new hot tub. We've only had the pool finished for two weeks but the three kids have been in it constantly, despite the June weather not being very summery yet. The hot tub is more my speed, even though the part of my body not covered by the boiling bubbles is still chilly. Luckily this is only over my shoulders because I'm not wearing a bathing suit. Even though the four of us in the hot tub share a very special relationship, I'm not one to sit up straight with boobies blazing, like Jacey does.

I'm not ashamed to admit she has better breasts than I do, either. Jacey has better breasts than anyone, even Melissa, and Melissa had work done on hers.

"I hadn't even thought of a pool," I say. "Neither of us did until Colin got that trampoline in the backyard. And then all we could think of is what we can do in the backyard."

"We can do lots of things in the backyard," Jackson leers.

"Yours *is* the biggest on the street," Jacey says.

"Why thank you," Jackson preens. "I didn't know you cared."

Jacey frowns. "It seems wrong for me to comment on the size of your penis in front of your wife."

"I was talking about my *backyard*," Jackson teases. "Get your mind out of the gutter, woman!"

"You don't want me talking about your penis?" she asks straight-faced.

I hold my breath. With Jacey, you can never be sure if she's joking or being completely serious.

But then she smiles. "It is a nice penis."

"And with that rousing attempt at enthusiasm..." Jackson mocks grumbles, before splashing water at Jacey. She instantly retaliates—a little too enthusiastically for four of us in such a small space – and the two of them begin a full-out water fight.

"Ah," Dominic cries, sounding like his six-year-old daughter. "Wendy, protect me!" He cuddles into my arms, hands brushing my breasts accidentally, and then again on purpose.

I laugh, taking the opportunity to hug Dominic close to me. His body is wider than Jackson's but firmer.

I wonder if I can say that about any other part of his anatomy.

Jackson glances over at us. Jacey is right – it still feels slightly taboo to talk openly about things like this, even though we have had sex with each other numerous times. Well, Dominic and Jackson haven't. And technically Jacey and I haven't either, although we have been in the same room. I think I'd like to with Jacey.

I think Jackson would too as well.

"Hey, I need some of that!" he decides and tries to pull Jacey over to him. She gives one last half-hearted attempt at splashing him before allowing herself to be drawn into his arms. "You can think about my penis any time you want," Jackson tells Jacey. "As long as my wife isn't thinking about it. She comes first." He blows me a kiss above the churning water. I know he's assuring me of his love – which I know will never change – and asking for my permission to take things further with Jacey.

We've been in the hot tub for about half an hour now and Jackson has been steadily inching closer to her among the bubbles. I don't think Jacey is opposed but probably wondering what's going on in my mind. It's one thing to watch your best friend smile and flirt with your husband *if* their husband isn't snuggled up just as close to you.

I guess she never realized my hand had been resting on Dominic's knee for most of the time we were in the hot tub. And now – ceasefire on the water fight – as Dominic draws away from my arms, he remains close beside me. Close enough to drape my legs over his lap.

I rub my leg questioningly where I think his penis should be and I'm rewarded by the feel of his hard cock jutting upright. I smile serenely at Jackson.

None of us wear bathing suits. When we invited Jacey and Dominic for dinner, we accidentally on purpose forgot to mention the idea about putting the kids to bed and hitting the hot tub. More importantly, we forgot to mention bringing bathing suits.

"Hot tub sounds like a great idea," Dominic had said enthusiastically when Jackson suggested it. "But we forgot our suits."

Dominic looked at Jacey, who glanced at me. Then she smiled at Jackson and started stripping down to her underwear in my kitchen. It had been awkward for about half a second. The kids were long asleep by then – Hanna and Ben upstairs with our three – and we were on our second bottle of wine.

We're moving steadily through this one as well. The hot tub had a nice area to keep wine glasses on.

Our clothes are now in a pile by the back door and I brought out some towels and a few thick hotel-style robes so we wouldn't have to streak in the cool night air. Jackson and Dominic did just that, however; running butt-naked through the backyard before jumping into the pool. Jacey and I had laughed at their screams from the warmth of the tub. I think Jacey would have been inclined to jump in as well, but I confessed to being too cold for such an act. I didn't mind watching the boys, though.

Before Jacey and Dominic moved in, we had always kept things confined to Tia's. Things such as having sex with our neighbours. We did it – but never at home. It was easy having your choice made for you. Tia picks a key; we get paired up. No hurt feelings; no uneasiness about getting picked, like in high school gym class. Saturday nights at Tia's, where we are guaranteed to have sex with someone other than our spouse. And I've never had a bad experience.

But now, after Jacey and Dominic moved in...

Jacey has to be the catalyst, but admittedly, I had thought about the possibility of being with Colin or Mahak or Joe...and now Nathan ...other than at Tia's, but never knew how to go about making that happen. Jacey is more sexually adventurous than anyone, even Melissa. I know Jacey had a few interludes with Mahak, and possibly with Tia. She doesn't like to kiss and tell like Melissa does, even though I'd be interested in what Jacey would have to say.

It's like her daringness is beginning to rub off on me. Tonight, I'm perfectly at ease with the four of us being naked together and excited about what's to come.

"What if we're both thinking about your penis?" I ask Jackson coyly, returning to the earlier discussion. I continue to rub Dominic's hardness under the water with my leg.

"Then I'm saying, *see ya* to my friend Dom here!" Jackson says immediately.

"You'd really diss me for the chance to have the both of them?" wonders Dominic. He drops his hands into my lap, stroking my thigh gently.

"Uh, hell ya! And you wouldn't?" Jackson says so quickly we laugh.

"Would you?" Jacey asks Dominic archly.

"Well, sure. It's every guy's fantasy to have two women, isn't it?" he says honestly, glancing between Jacey and me with an eager smile.

"Well, then," Jacey says slowly, and removing herself from Jackson's arms moves through the bubbling water towards me. I lick my lips. Is she – will she – *what's* she going to do?

She stands in front of me and I lift my face expectantly.

Dominic gives a low groan as Jacey leans down and kisses me softly on the lips. I reach up, my hands around her neck, just as she pulls away.

"I've been curious about that," she tells me.

"So have I!" Jackson cries, sounding frustrated. "In front of *me* next time!"

"No way, man," Dominic says, sounding dazed. "Again, please?"

"Nope. You've already had your chance," Jacey laughs at him, flicking water at her husband as she returns to Jackson.

Is that a pang of disappointment I feel?

"And so have you," I remind Jackson. Tia and Melissa. I think all the men have experienced Tia and Melissa because until not so long ago, they were the only ones willing.

I'm willing now.

"But that was so long ago," Jackson whines.

"Too bad," I tell him with a splash of my own. "You'll have to make do with one of us."

I glance over at Jacey and our eyes meet.

It's like we're giving each other permission.

"Aren't I enough for you?" Jacey asks him in a low voice, a voice that would make me excited if it was directed at me. She has no idea how sexy she is.

Instead of responding, Jackson pulls her onto his lap so she's straddling him. "Hope you don't mind?" he asks Dominic.

Dominic smiles as his hand drops between my legs.

"Hey, you can see right into Nathan's and Emma's kitchen from this angle," Jacey suddenly announces.

"You're sitting on my lap and you're watching the neighbours?" Jackson asks with disgust.

"You'll have to distract me a *little* more," Jacey tells him in that voice.

"I can do that," Jackson says eagerly.

"Have you done anything with them?" I ask Jacey.

"What do you mean?" she replies quickly. "Like this?" She waves an arm around the hot tub.

"Like dinner. Just dinner," I laugh. "Have you gotten to know them?"

"Well, I had sex with him at Tia's that time, but no, I don't really know them all that well," Jacey says wryly.

"I think that's one way of getting to know someone," Jackson grins.

"We had drinks with them that night," Dominic reminds her. "They seem nice."

"She's a bit uptight," Jacey says. "He seems cool. I've talked to him a few times."

Because I know Jacey, I can't help but wonder if talking was the only thing she did with him. Lucky Jacey. Since I first met Nathan, I haven't stopped hoping I'd get a chance with him. And now that we seem to have an agreement that things can proceed outside of Tia's...

I look over at Dominic, who is idly watching Jacey and Jackson with a smile on his face. What am I supposed to do now? I've never done this before. I never make the first move. Jackson and I have been together forever, but I rarely initiate things between us.

Dominic finally glances over at me with a smile. "I was just thinking that I'm getting a little cold," he says.

"Oh really?" My hand drifts to his cock, which doesn't feel affected by the temperature at all.

"I thought of making a fire," he continues, seemingly not bothered by my hand. I grip it firmly, stroking it under the water, out of sight. Dominic's only reaction is to close his eyes briefly.

I wonder what Dominic thinks about Jacey's adventures with the neighbours. He seems all right with it; she says he's fine, but you have to wonder what it's like for him to watch his wife being openly fondled by another man.

Actually, Jackson isn't openly groping her. I know what he's doing because I can tell by his face. Plus, I've been married to him long enough to know his moves. Not that they don't excite me, but they are predictable. Jacey's breasts are still submerged so I can only assume Jackson has two hands full. Jacey has beautiful breasts and my husband is very much a breast man.

After he has his fill of her breasts and plays with her nipples, his hands will wander down between her legs.

Jackson is the only man who has ever found my G-spot. His hands are large, his fingers long and quite dextrous. He can make me come in less than a minute if conditions are right.

Despite the openness of this relationship, I'm not ready to be around to see if he has the same effect on Jacey.

"A fire sounds great right about now," I tell Dominic. "I'm getting a bit cold myself."

"We can see that," Jackson says, gazing at my erect nipples above the bubbles.

"I do like your hot tub," Dominic says, pulling himself out of the water. I let my own gaze wander down his torso. Dominic is just a little more fit, a little firmer than Jackson and I do love the sight of a nice chest.

And then my gaze drops.

"So do I," Jacey says in a voice that is suddenly breathless.

Hand has reached pussy, I think. Or maybe it's the sight of her husband's rock-hard cock standing at attention getting her excited.

"We'll be inside," I say cheerily.

What do I think of my husband and another woman?

I'm not sure what you call it – are we swingers? Do we have an open marriage? The facts are that we enjoy our neighbours' company a little more than most. I'm not sure what that makes us, but I know for sure I'm a very satisfied woman.

And about to get even more satisfied.

"I've got to go check on the kids," I tell Dominic. He's wrapped himself in one of the robes I had laid out, perfect for this very occasion.

"Are you getting changed?" he wonders. I'm only wrapped in a towel.

"Should I?" I grin at Dominic's expression.

"Uh, no. Stay just like that. And maybe without the towel."

I smile in return. "You start the fire. I'll check on the kids."

My three kids were sleeping soundly; Hanna, Jacey and Dominic's daughter is curled up beside Faith and Ben flat on his back in Xander's room in the old Pac n' Play. When I come downstairs, Dominic hasn't made much headway with starting the fire.

"Do you know how to do that?" I wonder, trying to hide my smile as I watch him fumbling with the matches.

"I can do a lot of things. Starting a fire isn't one of them. But I thought I'd give it a try." He gives me an adorable grin. Dominic is so cute. He's the polar opposite of Jackson – stocky and solid rather than Jackson's lanky height.

Although I doubt I can call Jackson lanky any longer. He's been steadily gaining weight since we were married; not a lot, but enough to fill out his gangliness. Jackson will always be the tall, skinny geek I fell in love with in high school, all grown up to be my sexy and successful husband who happens to enjoy having sex with other women.

I like having sex with other men, so that makes it okay.

Dominic and I bring our glasses of wine in and I take a sip of before crouching beside Dominic in front of the fire. "Let me."

"Were you a Girl Scout or something?" he asks, amused by my take-charge manner.

"Girl Guide. All the way to Pathfinders. I got the all-around cord," I brag.

"I don't know what that means, but good for you."

"It means I'm always prepared," I say coyly, pulling out a condom from where I tucked it into the front of my towel.

"Why, Wendy," Dominic feigns shyness, "what kind of neighbour do you think I am?"

"The best kind," I whisper.

"What do you think they're doing?" he asks, standing behind me and massaging my bare shoulders. His touch distracts me from the business of getting the fire lit, but I don't want him to stop. His fingers dip into my cleavage and I have difficulty catching my breath.

"Same thing as we are."

"Are you okay with it? Them out there, us in here?" Dominic asks as I finally touch a match to the paper. It flames instantly and quickly catches the dry kindling. "You're good at this."

"I'm good at a lot of things," I joke. "You should know that."

"So you're cool?" he asks again.

"Aren't you? It's the same as when we're at Tia's. Just not as many people."

"I just wanted to make sure. We've never – you know – outside Tia's before."

"We fooled around before," I remind him. "Maybe this is getting to be a habit. You two over for dinner, kids asleep, things happening..."

"I remember," he smiles. "Do you...?" he trails off but I understand what he's getting at.

"I've never. Not outside Tia's. We've just..." I trail off as well, smiling shyly at him. "But when we invited you over, we thought maybe..."

"Really?"

I shrug, a little embarrassed at the thought of Dominic knowing we specifically invited them over for dinner to have sex with them. I don't know if that makes us swingers, or have an open marriage or what.

Maybe a little kinky. But I think that's okay. It works if everyone is happy with the arrangement.

"I feel so special," he says, moving closer.

Then he kisses me.

In my opinion, Dominic is the best kisser in the neighbourhood. Joe comes a close second but kissing Dominic makes me remember the make-out sessions in high school, back before things would go too far. When you could get excited just from the touch of a hand on bare skin.

I could go on happily kissing Dominic all night. Open mouth, but not too much tongue. Never too wet or messy – just perfect. I don't want him to stop kissing me.

But apparently, he has other plans. Or other places to kiss.

Dominic backs away, breaking the kiss, and when he does, my towel falls off. He takes a good, long admiring look as I pull my belly in as far as it can go, and wish my breasts are as full as Jacey's. Then he pushes me back onto the couch and drops to the floor before me.

"Oh," I say with surprise, as he bends my legs at the knees and pushes them up toward my chest before burying his face between them.

Mahak is the undisputed master of oral sex in the neighbourhood, so much that Jackson rarely bothers indulging me. But Dominic – Dominic comes in a close second.

I lean back against the couch and put my hands on the back of his curly head as the tip of his tongue traces between my folds, slowly delving deeper.

Jackson would have – don't compare them. That's the main thing you have to remember. Never compare, just enjoy.

And I enjoy myself. Dominic begins to tongue my clit gently, with teasing little flickers and my breath hitches. Then he kisses me between flicks, at the same time sliding a finger inside me. I've been excited since he and Jacey got here, unable to stop thinking about what might happen. It's the same Saturday nights at Tia's. I get so turned on with the anticipation, of what I imagine is going to happen, it usually doesn't take much to make me come.

I don't think it's going to take long tonight.

Dominic plunges another finger inside me as his mouth finds my clit and sucks it. I gasp because it feels so good and he does it again, harder this time.

It's hard to keep quiet.

Between tongue and fingers and mouth, Dominic keeps me on the edge for long minutes. Every time I'm about to dissolve into an orgasm, he changes direction or pressure. Soon I'm begging for it. Begging for him to make me come.

And with a long last suck on my clit, I come, stifling my cry in my hands. But Dominic doesn't stop, making me writhe on the couch, my hands clutching the back of his head as I pull him into me to take more in his mouth.

He complies, removing his fingers only to thrust his tongue inside me, before attacking my clit with a barrage of firm tongue lashes.

"Oh, God," I whimper, doing my best to keep quiet.

His fingers are back inside me, and his tongue – oh my god, his tongue. I can't keep quiet, I can't keep still as I feel the second orgasm build within me. Waves of pleasure are coursing through me, starting from the tips of my toes, through my arms and legs –

As he sucks on my clit once more, his fingers find the secret spot inside me and I explode with a sharp cry.

Dominic moves above as I'm still awash with sensations and kisses me deeply. I can taste myself on his mouth and I'm not conscious of anything else but the feel of him in my arms and how my body is still tingling. Then he thrusts into me so quickly that I gasp.

"I'm sorry, but I have to fuck you now," he says.

It's like my orgasm never ends. I was still cresting on the wave when it starts to build again as he fucks me hard and fast, pulling out once to position my legs against his shoulders. Dominic is like a man possessed, in and out, in and out, his eyes focused above me, a few damp curls flopping onto his forehead. I put my hand on his chest and he makes a growling sound.

But there's no time for me to come again because Dominic thrusts even harder now, eyes closed and hands gripping my hips. I can tell when he comes because his face contorts and it's like he's expelling all the air in his body. And then he smiles.

"Sorry," he says quietly as he pulls out. "I couldn't wait any longer."

"No need to apologize," I assure him, feeling dazed. As I watch, he pulls off the condom. I hadn't even noticed he put it on.

"You can't leave her like that," a quiet voice says. I whirl around to see Jacey and Jackson standing behind the couch where they have a bird's eye view of what Dominic and I have been doing.

"Have you been there the whole time?" I gasp. I snatch the towel to cover myself.

"I should have said something," Dominic says sheepishly. "They only saw the last few minutes."

"I hope you don't mind," Jacey says, moving around the couch and touching my arm. "I was thinking maybe we could finish what we started in the hot tub. If you're up for it?" she says in a low voice.

I look at her hand on my arm and then into her eyes. She has beautiful eyes. I drop the towel, take her face in my hands and kiss her.

"Oh, man," I hear Jackson groan. "We need to take this back outside."

I pull away from Jacey. "People will see us."

"All the lights are out," Jacey assures me.

"And people should really see this," Jackson says, motioning to Jacey and me. "Let's go for a little swim."

"I went down on Jackson in the hot tub," Jacey confesses. "I want to see if I can do it to you."

"I don't want you to drown," I laugh.

"What a way to go," Dominic says.

We head back outside to the pool where Dominic and Jackson, both wrapped in robes, settle themselves on the lounges pulled close to the edge of the water. Jacey drops her towel by the edge and slowly steps into the water, grimacing when the cool water touches her skin. Conscious of all three watching me, I stride to the deep end and stand poised at the lip. I had been on the swim team in high school so if there is one thing I am comfortable with in this situation, it's my skills in the water.

Honestly, it's about the only thing right now. Nerves mix with excitement, making my belly churn.

"Go for it, baby," Jackson encourages me, and I execute a perfect swan dive into the water, surfacing at the brink of the shallow end.

Jacey is still struggling to make it down the stairs. I emerge from the water, water streaming off me like some sort of mermaid, and take her hand.

"It's nice when you get in," I tell her, helping her down the steps.

"Maybe we should go back to the hot tub," she grumbles. The water reaches her waist and she keeps her arms up.

"I'll warm you up," I promise and grasping her arms, pull her through the water towards me.

I've always been intrigued at the thought of being with another woman, and thanks to Melissa's lessons in girl-on-girl etiquette, I feel surprisingly at ease kissing Jacey again in the pool with our husbands watching. Dominic had satisfied me, but these days I'm always ready for more.

Jacey's lips are cool and soft. Kissing a woman is different than kissing a man. Lips are softer, and more pliable. I can gauge what a woman wants more easily than I can a man. With a man, I like to let them take charge. With a woman, I feel like we're equal partners.

Of course, I've only ever been with two women, Melissa and Tia. And now Jacey.

Despite my plunge into the cool water, Jacey eagerly wraps her arms around me as our lips meet. She's only a few inches taller than I am, and our bodies are a good fit. Her curves are a sharp contrast to my slender frame and feel good as I stroked her bare back.

Jacey doesn't waste any time and immediately reaches for my breasts.

The backyard is in darkness and the only light comes from the kitchen window and the bright, almost full moon above. Jackson has turned off the pool lights so Jacey and I are dark silhouettes in the water. Jackson and Dominic sit close enough to watch but I'm hoping no one else is. The houses surrounding us are in darkness.

Jacey and I kiss for long moments, enjoying the feel of each others' mouths, caressing each others' breasts. The only sounds are the slight movement of the water and Jackson's hum of appreciation until Jacey moans as my fingers pull on her nipple.

"This is really hot, girls, but would you please get on with it?" Jackson asks in a hoarse voice.

"Patience, man," Dominic chides him. "Don't rush them."

"How can you be patient watching this?" Jackson retorts in a pained voice. "I've waited my whole life to see this!"

I pull away from Jacey and laugh. "He has no patience with things like this," I say.

"He sees what he wants and goes and gets it?" Jacey asks. "I've got one of those but he's got a little more willpower."

"I'm doing my best not to jump in the pool there with you, so will you shush up," Jackson says through gritted teeth, making us laugh.

"What do you want to see, big boy?" Jacey taunts. "Want to see these?" She moves over to the edge of the pool, holding her full breasts in her hands, leaning over the edge to where Jackson is sitting. "Want to have a touch?" But when my husband reaches out an eager hand, she darts back into the water, her arms quickly covering herself. "Nah, nah, you had your turn. It's Wendy's turn now."

"Lucky me," I grin.

Jacey beckons me over to the corner of the pool, right by the stairs. She sits me down on the top stair, so I'm sitting in a puddle of water that would barely cover my foot. And then she kneels on the steps in front of me.

"We really have to thank Melissa for this, you know," she says with a smile.

"Yes, we do," I agree, spreading my legs wide.

Jacey positions one of my legs on the step beside me and I glance up at the house beside us. If Colin or Paige were to look out their window into our backyard, they would have a perfect view of my pussy.

Jackson and Dominic try to hitch their loungers closer to get a better view, but can't get close enough. "Fuck this," Jackson says with frustration, standing up and shedding his robe. Then he jumps in the water with a splash as Jacey crouches over my pussy.

Just as I think I'm about to feel her mouth, she pulls back. "Do you like to touch yourself?" she asks.

"What?"

"Touch yourself. Play with yourself. I've never seen anyone do that."

"And it has to be me?" But I do as she asks, running a finger along my cleft, feeling my own wetness.

"I'm getting closer for this," I heard Dominic mutter, splashing through the water beside Jackson.

I look at Jacey, at the three of them avidly watching me play with myself and the sight of them gets me as excited as my own fingers are making me. I add a finger, stroking myself slowly, languidly, thrusting inside before moving to my clit.

"This is kind of hot," Jacey says. Her eyes focus on my glistening pussy, my fingers rubbing the hard nub of my clit.

And it is. My breath speeds up as I circle the sensitive spot, harder and faster. Kissing Jacey, thinking about what she was going to do to me has already gotten me so excited. It won't take me long at all.

"Is this how you make yourself come?" Jacey asks. "Can you do it now?"

"I'd rather have you do it," I tell her honestly.

"In a minute," she says, still staring.

"It's only going to take me a minute," I say, slipping a finger inside and searching for my G-spot.

"Yeah, she's quick," Jackson agrees.

I return to my clit as Jacey moves closer, touching my inner thighs with cool fingers. Her heavy breasts hang low, almost touching the water, her nipples hard with either cold or excitement. I reach out and cup her breast, rolling the nipple between my fingers as I play with myself.

"Oh, my fuck," Jackson groans as Jacey leans over me, adding her tongue to the pressure on my clit. I take my hand away, leaning back on my arms as she begins to tongue me.

Long, slow, wet licks reaching into every part of my pussy. Then she attacks my clit with flickers of her tongue, firm enough to make me cry out.

"I need to fuck your wife," Jackson says to Dominic, splashing through the water to stand behind Jacey.

"Again?" Dominic asks. "I was thinking of doing that."

"You can have her anytime. She only gave me a blow job earlier."

"What, am I just supposed to watch?"

I can feel Jacey's intake of breath against my pussy as Jackson slides into her. Almost immediately she begins to moan as Jackson thrusts hard against her and she shifts position so she's on all fours on the steps.

"Wendy," Jackson grunts. I don't know if he is talking to me or telling Dominic to go to me, but I hold out a hand to Dominic and he quickly climbs out of the pool to stand beside me. He dropped his robe before he jumped in and I caress his thigh before grasping his cock in my hand.

"Oh, god," I moan as Jacey increases the pressure on my clit. I lean up and take Dominic's cock in my mouth. Usually, I would take the time to tease, circling the tip with my tongue, scraping my teeth ever so slowly along the length, just the way Jackson likes it. I like giving blow jobs and I'm told I'm very good at it. But Jacey is going to make me come quickly and I don't have time to waste.

I moan, my mouth full of Dominic and he presses the back of my head so that I take him all the way in until he touches the back of my throat. Jacey is making muffled noises, a vibration that adds to the pleasure of her tongue. She focuses on my clit, licking in circles, slowly speeding up before flicking just the tip, and the sides, and licking my entire cleft.

I can feel an orgasm building quickly, like listening to the conversation of people walking towards you. I grasp Dominic's balls in one hand, grabbing hold of his leg with my other as I bob my head frantically along the length of him. Dominic reaches down and takes the base of his shaft in his hand, rubbing it with jerky strokes as I concentrate on the head of his cock.

"Oh, fuck..." Jackson groans loudly and I know he's about to come. Jacey can't stop making noises, which makes her mouth feel so good against my pussy.

"I'm going to come," I cry out, muffled by Dominic's cock. The rush of sensations race through my body, towards my core and the release I need. Jacey thrusts her fingers inside me at the same time as she sucks on my clit and I explode with a harsh cry, pressing my pussy against her face.

Almost in unison, Jackson comes with a grunt and I see Jacey convulse in the water as her own orgasm takes control of her body. And then it's Dominic's turn to empty himself into my mouth and I swallow every drop.

"Holy fuck," Jackson says as he heaves himself out of Jacey and collapses into the water.

"You really need to learn some new vocabulary words for sex," Jacey tells him, sitting back in the water and dunking her head.

"Yeah, but it fits," Jackson argues. "You're all thinking the same thing."

"I know I am," Dominic says as I lean back onto my arms again, trying to slow my breathing. "Thanks for inviting us for dinner," he grins, pulling on a robe and tying it around his waist. I stand up and grope for my towel.

"Thanks for dessert," I grin.

Colin

"WE REALLY NEED A pool," I mutter to myself, resting my head against the cool glass of the window, my cock in my hand. I've been watching the four of them – Dominic, Jacey, Jackson and Wendy – get it on in Jackson's new pool. I'd never seen anything like that before. Jacey going down on Wendy in the water, with Jackson fucking her from behind and Wendy sucking Dominic's dick? "Why don't they ever invite us over?"

I glance over to where Paige is sleeping sweetly, curled up on her side, wearing one of my oversized T-shirts. It's pulled up to reveal an expanse of the smooth thigh and half of her grabbable ass.

I'm an ass man, in more ways than one, and my wife has a great one.

She also has a habit of not wearing underwear to bed.

The way I look at it, I have two options here. Watching the four of them behave like something out of a porno film has got me so horny – too horny to go back to sleep without doing something about it. So I can take myself into the bathroom with a box of Kleenex or I can wake up Paige.

Or I could try *not* to wake her up.

Paige it is. It's not a difficult decision. Paige has always been willing and eager, especially lately, ever since Jacey moved in. That girl is a bad influence on our entire neighbourhood but in the best possible way. Sure, Paige and I went through a bad patch years ago, but that's all forgiven now.

Now, not being able to keep my dick in my pants isn't a bad thing because Paige is doing the same thing. We've been keeping things at Tia's but watching the two couples in the pool makes me wonder if it's time things can be taken out of the party situation. There was that time with Jacey in the kitchen, but that had been a quickie and who could blame me? She had come on so strong – no man could have resisted. Jacey is *sexy*.

But so is my wife and she's right here. I keep the image of Jacey on her knees in the water in my mind as I lay down carefully behind Paige, doing my best not to wake her up. She's laying in the fetal position, with the sheet pushed off and her bare ass only inches from my wandering fingers.

I began stroking the back of her legs ever so gently with the tips of my fingers, right where the thigh meets the ass, following the curve of her buttocks until I could feel the heat from her pussy. Paige had been talking about the possibility of a Brazilian wax job for our next vacation or even going completely bare, but I like my women with a little bush.

Melissa has the hairiest pussy I've ever seen. That has always surprised me, based on how much Mahak likes to go down on her. I assume he likes it. It's all I hear about from the ladies.

I have no idea why I'm thinking about Melissa's pussy at this moment. Maybe because it's always tight and wet and ready...

But so is Paige.

And so is Jacey.

I couldn't help but think of one of my favourite neighbours as my fingers moved closer to Paige's pussy. I'd been with Jacey three times now and each had been memorable. The first time at Tia's – she let me slide into her ass; the threesome with Jackson for her birthday; and only a few weeks ago, a quickie in my own kitchen while Paige and Dominic were right outside with the kids. Jacey is something else, but watching her with the others tonight, I saw something new. She's always ready to go, but she seemed more wanton tonight. Shameless. The four of them in the pool where anyone can see.

It is well after midnight though and for the most part, the residents of Honeysuckle Court are the early-to-bed, early-to-rise sort of folks.

Ready to rise for every occasion, I smile to myself, glancing down at my rampant cock. If I move only a little, I can slip right into Paige before she wakes up.

No. This will be more fun. I slide a hand between her legs until I touch her slick folds. And then I begin stroking, lightly with a teasing caress so she barely notices.

I want to make her come while she's sleeping.

The angle she's sleeping in is perfect. Great access. I slip a finger inside her warmth, thrusting gently and waiting for the wetness to begin. A second finger, firmer thrusts. After a little of this finger fucking, I go for the clit, rubbing the nub as gently as I can, but hard enough to make sure Paige feels it. I circle with two fingers, the way she likes it. Paige has the most responsive pussy. She's not as quick to come as Wendy, but she's not too far behind.

It takes forever to make Melissa come. Probably because she's never shy about barking out instructions. Paige just lies back and enjoys herself, which I like. I like her to enjoy herself.

Why am I thinking of Melissa?

Paige's breathing changes. I'm not sure if she's awake, but her body is beginning to respond to my touch. I increase the pressure on her clit and speed up a little.

I start a rhythm – clit, and then move to fingers inside her pussy, and then back to her clit. I can tell she likes that because she's thrusting her hips forward slightly.

I'm getting excited too. I wonder if I can make her come before she wakes up. And then be inside her when she does wake up?

With my other hand, I caress the cheek of her ass as I run my thumb in the crevasse until I find her puckered little asshole. This would be good tonight. I can go for this. While I suspect going in the backdoor isn't Paige's first preference, she never complains. We've never discussed it, but I'll say she enjoys it, and that's not just wishful thinking.

I move back to her clit, pinching it gently between my fingers, rubbing in a circular motion, the same way Paige does it when I watch her masturbate.

Yep. Paige will do just about anything for me. I'm a lucky man. But I think it's helped me learn a lot about what a woman wants.

Paige's breathing is coming in little gasps now and I want to check if her eyes are open. But even if she's awake, she's not saying anything to stop me. My fingers move faster around her clit, then thrust back inside. I'm not as gentle now. My thumb caresses her asshole and I push forward, feeling the resistance of the muscles. Using some of her own wetness as lubrication, I circle her ass and then push my thumb inside her, slowly and carefully until the sphincter releases me and I'm through. I keep rubbing her clit and feel her body responding, jerking her hips forward, her breath coming in little gasps.

That's the secret, I've found. A woman will do just about anything if you get her excited enough. And never leave her unsatisfied.

My thumb thrusts in her ass and my fingers are going crazy on her clit. I'm not being careful anymore. I can't wait for her to come. I can't wait to fuck her.

Paige is close; I can tell. She makes a soft keening noise as she arches her back and thrusts her hips forward – then with a shiver that's almost a convulsion, she comes, my fingers frantically rubbing until I know she's spent.

And then I move closer and slide my cock into her waiting pussy. So warm, so wet.

Grabbing her hips, I pull her backwards, angling her for a better angle. It's my hands on her hips that finally break the spell.

"Colin?" she says weakly.

"Who else are you expecting?" I grin into her hair, moving against her.

She laughs softly and gives a little gasp as I pull out and slam into her roughly. "Nice way to wake up."

"I tried to be gentle for as long as I could," I apologize. "Done with that now. This is the way you like it, right?"

Paige makes a sound of assent in her throat. I move my thumb back to her ass. "And you like this, right? Can I do this?"

I feel her head nod this time, and without wasting time, I pull out of her pussy and begin to nudge my cock against her ass. Slowly and carefully as to not hurt her, I press inside until my head is through.

I hear Paige's intake of breath, and then I slide all the way in. "Okay?" I whisper. She nods again, and I start to move within her, loving the tightness around my cock.

I like the position—spooning with her back pressed against my chest, but it's not letting me be as hard as I want. So I pull out and roll Paige on her stomach, tugging her hips up so she's on her knees, ass in the air, and head on the pillow.

"I won't be long," I promise. I'm not sure if the girls talk about it, but I suspect I'm the quickest draw on the street. I just can't help myself. The feel of a woman, my cock clasped within her grip...

"I don't mind," Paige replies breathlessly, and I slide carefully inside her once more, waiting for the little gasp, the slight relaxation that tells me the worst is over and she's beginning to enjoy it. Then I begin to fuck her, not as hard as I do when I'm in her pussy, but forceful enough to have my balls swinging between her legs. I reach around and begin to finger her clit again. No woman I've ever been with has reached an orgasm with a dick in her ass, but I was brought up right.

Never leave them unsatisfied.

Paige gives a little moan as I touch her clit with my finger. She cries out as I furiously rub the sensitive nub and push her hips back against me.

Luckily, happily, for me, Paige doesn't take long for the second round. Either I'm hitting the spot with my finger and cock, or this excites her more than she tells me. But just as it's becoming uncomfortable for me, and I'm thinking I can't hold out much longer, she gives a sharp cry and I can feel the shiver of her body.

That's all I need and with a groan of my own, I empty myself into her.

"What was that all about?" Paige asks after I collapse on the bed beside her.

"I woke up and saw you...couldn't help myself," I say, then I decide to tell her the truth. "I went pee and looked out the window. I saw Wendy and Jackson and Dominic and Jacey. In the pool. Together."

"So?" she rolls over to look at me with sleepy confusion.

"*Together*," I repeat with a wiggle of my eyebrows.

She gets it this time. "Really? All four of them?"

I nod, feeling the relaxation of a good orgasm hit me, and realizing I'm not going to be awake much longer.

"We've never done that," Paige surprises me by saying.

"Would you want to?"

She shrugs into the pillow. "Why not?" And then she snuggles her face into the crook of my neck. I wrap my arm around her as she kisses my neck. "Going back to sleep. Thanks for the wake-up call."

I have the best wife.

Nathan

I BUMP INTO WENDY on the street outside our houses when I return from my run today.

Considering what I had witnessed her doing with Jackson, Jacey and Dominic the other night in their pool, it's a little awkward for me. Not for her, because obviously, she has no idea I was standing at the window in the hallway, watching the four of them play in the pool. I had to wake up Emma after that.

I haven't had much to do with our neighbours since we moved in, other than that first party at Tia's. I guess there was Melissa's brunch where we got the invite to Tia's and then drinks with Jacey and Dominic that one night. I had sex with Jacey, but that's not always the best way to get to know someone. I think she's pretty cool, though. Other than Jacey, I haven't had much to do with the neighbours.

They all seem pretty nice. Interesting that they've turned out to be a big group of swingers. I never would have expected that.

I never would have expected Emma and me to be involved with that either. *Especially* Emma.

But it is a good way to get to know the neighbours and I think we could use the social aspect and the relationship. Emma's a teacher, so it's not like she can hang out with the other ladies during the day. I'm around the house more than she is, with my schedule at the fire station being four days on, and four days off.

Emma's never really been one to have close friends, and over the years, I've let most of mine fall by the wayside. Lazy, I guess, or because I got married years before they did and missed out on all the single guy stuff they were into. But getting some new friends out of this deal isn't a bad thing.

"Hi," Wendy says with surprise. "Out for a run?"

My T-shirt is sweaty and sticking to me. "Yep. How's the new pool? I've been watching the construction."

Now, why would I mention the pool? Should I just go ahead and tell her I was playing Peeping Tom the other night and get it over with?

"It's great," Wendy says. "The kids love it. I hope it didn't disturb you guys too much."

"No worries. Em's at work all day and nothing really bothers me. It was nice hearing the kids play yesterday."

Will you shut up about the stupid pool? I tell myself. But I'm not listening to myself.

"Perfect weather to lie around a pool," I say. "Lie in the sun, work on your tan."

Wendy holds up her arm. "I'm pretty pasty."

"I'm not saying...tanning is bad for your skin," I say hastily, realizing I've put my foot in my mouth again. "Skin cancer, and all that."

"You should really be careful," she says, touching my arm with hers to see the comparison.

"Wow, you're cold," I say in surprise.

"Melissa has the air con cranked. It was freezing inside. I'd rather keep the windows open. Wow," she continues ruefully. "Cold *and* pasty."

"Porcelain skin," I correct "Pale. Ethereal skin. Not pasty. And blessedly cool."

"I was joking," she tells me with a smile.

"Oh! Good. Sometimes I have foot-in-mouth disease and –"

"Don't worry. I'm used to Jacey. Sometimes her filter doesn't work. If she even has one."

"Jacey..." I murmur, my mind racing to the sight of Jacey crouched in the pool, her head between Wendy's legs.

"Your neighbour?" Wendy supplies.

"Oh, I know who she is," I say, a bit too heartily because Wendy blanches. "I mean – can we start over?" I ask in a rush. "Nothing I say is coming out right. I think you must be intimidating me."

"How can *I* possibly intimidate *you*?"

Slowly, I look Wendy up and down, being really obvious about it. "Well, just look at you," I tell her with a shy smile.

Her face softens briefly, her mouth opening to a delighted little O before she laughs. "Oh, you're good," she says.

"I'm deadly serious," I say. And I really am, despite the corniness of my delivery. Wendy is a very good-looking woman. I like how her tight, black shorts accentuate her long, still very pale, legs.

"You're forgetting I'm married to Jackson," Wendy continues. "He's the biggest flirt on the street."

"I can't blame him. There are all these beautiful, sexy women to talk to..."

"You should go talk to Mrs. Stein," Wendy points to the house on the corner across from Tia's.

"How can she be anything less than lovely if she lives here?"

"She's probably in her eighties by now. She'd love you – big, strapping fireman come to visit her."

I make a face. She doesn't know about..."

Wendy cuts me off with a laugh. "I'm sure she'd have a heart attack if she knew what went on at Tia's. In fact, I haven't seen her in a while," she muses. "Someone should really check on her."

"I'm pretty good with CPR," I tell her. "Rather not use it on my neighbours, though."

"How about playing lifeguard?" Wendy suggests.

"I was a lifeguard in high school," I say promptly.

"That was my way of asking if you want to come over for a swim," she says. "You're all hot and sweaty, I need to warm up..."

"Oh! That sounds great. Thanks. But I really can't today," I say, backing away from her.

"Too bad," she says lightly.

"Yeah. Definitely. But Emma was running late this morning and forgot her lunch and I said I'd run it over to the school for her."

"That's sweet of you."

"I'm a sweet guy."

"I think so," Wendy says, with an appraising glance that is the perfect blend of obvious and joking. Or maybe she's just joking? "Well, there's always this afternoon. I wouldn't mind the company."

"Really?" I didn't want to ask about Jacey, Melissa, or Paige. I would think they would be better company. "I should be able to help you with that."

"I bet you can," she says with a sly smile.

"Ok. So I'll stop by later when I get back. With my suit..."

"If you like," she says off-handedly. "I'll leave the door open."

That stops me in my tracks. I don't think it was *me* she sounded so nonchalant about.

I think it's me bringing a bathing suit over to swim.

Holy shit.

Was it an invitation? I don't know Wendy well enough to know. Her pretty face is expressionless. And I will definitely look even more of an ass if I ask.

What the hell?

I know these neighbours aren't the usual kind that brings over cookies and casseroles when you move in, then never says more than boo to you, except for fake conversation about the weather over the fence in the backyard. That's what it was like in our old place, and that's what I expected here. It's the reason I hate the suburbs. So many neighbours and no one taking the time to get to know each other, unless there are kids and play dates involved.

Kids aren't in the cards for us.

I grew up in the city and my parents had friends in our neighbourhood; friends who came over for dinner – real dinner, not just the obligatory neighbourhood barbeque one keen soul inevitably throws. And whose kids weren't the same age or sex, but still played together, even though they might ignore each other in school.

That had been Robin Dawson for me. Our parents were best friends and we spent countless Saturday nights together playing or watching television while our parents laughed and drank bottles of wine, but she would never talk to me in school.

Too bad. I had the biggest crush on her. I even kissed her when I was thirteen. Unfortunately, after that, her parents deemed her old enough to stay at home by herself when the Dawson's came over and I hardly saw her again.

After I take Emma's lunch to her at the school, I go home and putter around the house for a while. I don't tell Emma about Wendy's invitation to swim, mainly because I'm confused about it. On paper, it seems innocent enough. It's a hot day, she has a new pool. But the comment about bringing a suit and leaving the door open makes me wonder.

I don't have a lot of experience with women. I had girlfriends before Emma but they were the long-term, monogamous kind. I was twenty-four when Em and I got married so during the twenty-something years typically spent getting as much pussy as possible, I was a husband.

Not that I'm complaining. I love Emma more than anything, but it's hard wanting to try new things and continually having to persuade her with talk of safety and pleasure, with the use of pictures and promises. Emma likes knowing what's going on, what's going to happen, how and why. She likes being in control of any situation. Spontaneity is not on her list of characteristics, and neither is being open to exploring her sexuality. Most times it's easier to take no for an answer, leaving me to get my kicks from the porn I have to hide from my wife.

Until now. Not that I still don't have to hide my porn collection, but with neighbours like these, I'll never want for adventure again. Look at what I get from just the window. First watching Jacey, and then peaking at what was going on at Wendy's...is it any wonder why I'm confused with her invitation?

With the image of Wendy and Jacey in my mind, I change into my bathing suit and head over to Wendy's. I have to wear a suit. I can't imply I'm there for something other than a swim, just a swim.

Even though I'd be lying if I said I'm not up for something more. Yes, I am thinking about seeing Wendy naked again. Does that make me a bad neighbour? Actually, I think it means I fit in perfectly around here.

I head over to Wendy's, repeatedly looking over my shoulder in case I see anyone. Not that I'm doing anything wrong. Wendy was nice enough to invite me over for a swim. I have every intention of telling Emma.

But I'd rather no one else tell her first.

I knock on the door, but there's no answer. As I'm standing there, wondering to take Wendy on her word and walk in, I hear a sharp cry. The windows on the upper floor are open and as I'm looking around to see where the source is, I hear another cry from inside.

"Wendy?" I call and check the door, which is unlocked. I rush in, fireman senses on full alert.

There's a moan and another cry. "Wendy? Are you ok?"

Upstairs. I take the steps two at a time, frantically wondering what I'll find. Is she hurt – has she fallen or is she injured or incapacitated in some way –

I check the bedrooms and the bathroom. Kids' bedrooms with stuffed animals and LEGO and pastel-coloured walls.

Then I find Wendy.

It must be the master bedroom; Jackson and Wendy's room with a huge bed that is covered with a dark duvet and stacks of pillows. Wendy is sprawled on the bed, feet propped up on the edge.

She's uh—playing with herself.

I bite back anything I'm about to say because really, what do you say when faced with such a picture?

And what a picture.

Wendy's eyes are closed and she's completely focused on what she's doing between her legs. It takes a moment until I realize she's got a tiny, very quiet vibrator in her hand.

I should leave. I should back away and go downstairs and out the door. That would be the polite, the *neighbourly* thing to do. Unfortunately, I'm frozen in the doorway. I can't tear my eyes away from the sight of Wendy's pussy, pink and glistening, hips thrusting upward. One hand is between her legs and the other is toying with her nipple. I've never seen anything like this, other than in some movie, but this is *real*. This is a real woman in the midst of pleasuring herself. This is Wendy, my neighbour, who I watched give Dominic a blowjob while Jacey ate her out while Jackson fucked her.

This is Wendy, who has quickly become some sort of sex goddess to me. It's like I'm Peter Pan and she's my Wendy Darling.

I once watched an X-rated version of Peter Pan. Wendy and Peter Pan, while Tinkerbell did the Lost Boys. I'll probably never be able to watch the original movie ever again.

Wendy moans again and my cock is rock hard.

I back away. I back away because if I'm not going in there with Wendy and helping her out, then I need to go. As hot as watching her is, it will be beyond awkward if she opens her eyes and sees me standing there. But how can I leave her like this? Why would I want to?

I back away from the door, stifling my own moan.

I continue to watch her until I'm halfway down the hall and Wendy is lost from sight. Then I turn and rush down the stairs, forgetting to be quiet in my need for haste.

"Hello?" Wendy calls, surprised and somewhat breathlessly. "Is there someone here?"

Apparently, I'm not quiet at all.

"Uh—it's Nathan. I've come—I'm here to swim like you invited me over for? I can come—I can go if it's a bad time or if you're busy with—"

I hear her chuckle.

"I'll be right down. I'm just—changing. Do you need to get your suit on?

'No, I'm uh, wearing it."

"Because you can use one of the rooms up here if you want to."

"I'm good," I call back.

I stand politely, obediently by the door, like I'm not the sort of man who would enter a house uninvited and walk right upstairs. Not the sort of man who would stand by and watch a woman masturbate.

I thought she was injured. I was only doing what any Good Samaritan would do.

You'd think I'd be able to distinguish cries of pleasure from cries of pain. I've seen and heard enough on the screen, but my reality is that Emma is pretty quiet.

"Hi," Wendy says as she comes down the stairs. Her face is flushed and she's smiling and wearing a bikini that leaves little to the imagination.

I no longer need my imagination.

"Ready?" she says.

"For—for what?" I stammer.

"To swim?" she frowns and gestures to my trunks. Instinctively, my hands slap in front of my crotch. Jesus, I'm still hard and it's sticking up! "Isn't that why you're wearing your bathing suit?"

"Uh, sure, of course. Swim. With you. Just swim."

"You okay, Nathan?" Wendy asks, her head cocked to the side and a hint of a smile on her pretty face.

"Yep. Just fine." I do my best to keep looking her in the eye, instead of at those perky little tits in the halter-style top or where I know her pink and pretty pussy is hiding under the brief bottoms. I know for a fact she has had a Brazilian...

"Want a drink?" she offers, and I wrench my eyes up again. Jesus, I should just go before I make an ass of myself.

"If this is a bad time..." I try but Wendy waves my attempt away.

"Of course not. I'll be glad for the company. So—drink?"

"Sure." Maybe a cold shower would be better, I think to myself. Or cold pool water. I've got to do something with this hard-on because it's really embarrassing and not going away –

I follow Wendy into the kitchen and when she stops suddenly, I run into her.

"Sorry!" I gasp my hands on her bare back. There's only a moment where I'm touching her skin, but it's warm and smooth and does absolutely nothing to help the erection go away.

Wendy turns to face me, standing unnecessarily close. And then she moves even closer, so close that her breasts are almost touching my chest. When she touches me—hands reaching for my shoulder and sliding to rest on my biceps—I almost groaned aloud.

"So you're a fireman," she says lightly. I can barely manage a nod. "You're in good shape."

"I'm sure Jackson is in just good as shape as me," I tell her, pulling my hips back so I have more space between my hard cock and her smooth belly.

Wendy only smiles. "Did you hear me upstairs?"

She puts a hand right on my dick and I swallow with an audible gulp.

"I saw you," I confess. I can deny it, but what's the point? I hang my head in shame but also so I can watch her stroke my hardness through my shorts.

Which she's doing, with a slow, yet firm stroke. Then she rubs the tip with her thumb and I can't help it this time – a low groan escapes.

"You did, did you? Dirty boy."

I look down at her face –so pretty and so sweet and talking like a two-bit whore. "Do you like dirty boys?" I ask in a low voice.

"Do you like watching me play with myself?"

I gesture to her hand, still stroking me. "I think you can see that for yourself."

"I like that you like it."

"I like that you like that I like that," I say, stumbling a little over the words.

Wendy laughs, and then sighs, giving me a little squeeze through my shorts. "Do you really want to go for a swim right now?"

"Not unless it's with you and you're wearing a lot less than what you are right now," I say truthfully. "But then your neighbours might see and wonder what's going on."

"You're my neighbour. Do you wonder what's going on?"

"I think I've figured out what's going on. At least I think so. I know what was going on the other night."

Wendy's eyes widened with alarm. I lean forward, grasp her hips and yank her forward. "I like to watch," I say in such a low voice it's almost a growl. "I like to watch you. If you think I'm hard now—" I grind myself against her hand still caught between us, "—you should have seen me that night. I don't know if anything has made me as horny as watching you and Jacey."

"Really?" she whispers.

"Except maybe watching you upstairs. When you didn't know I was there."

"I knew you were there," she tells me, her eyes lowered. "I wanted you to catch me. I just thought we'd be doing this upstairs."

I look around the kitchen. "This is just as good a place." Then I kiss her roughly enough for both of us to lose our breath.

I'm always so careful with Emma because she's so tiny and still so afraid of sex. When I kiss her, when I touch her, it's like she's a porcelain doll and I'm afraid of breaking her. When I do get rough, it scares her and I'm back to square one.

When I kiss Wendy, it's with mouth open, tongue probing and it's good. I don't remember the last time I kissed with that much intensity.

Wendy's body is just as slender as Emma's, but she's got her arms around me just as tight as I do. Her body is telling me she wants me just as much as I want her, which makes me want her so much more.

But then I have one last moment of clarity. Emma. Jackson. Neighbours.

"Are you sure this is okay?" I ask as I break to catch my breath.

"God, yes," Wendy gasps, sliding her hands down the back of my bathing trunks to grasp my ass.

Even the thin material of our bathing suits is too much of a barrier. I fumble with the knots of her bikini top and manage to get the one at the back of her head undone, and I push the fabric down to feel her bare breasts against my chest. I slide my hands along the length of her torso so I can cup her breasts – small and soft and not quite as firm as Emma's but still nice. My fingers find her nipples and Wendy lets out a gasp, our mouths still pressed together.

She's pressed her hips against me so there's no room for my hand in the front. I reach around, sliding my hand under the elastic of her bikini bottom, over her ass, my long fingers searching for her warm wetness.

I need more of her. I yank down her bottoms and lift her onto the counter. She quickly unties the last knot and her bikini top falls to the floor.

I'm tall, so the position works. I push down my shorts enough to pull my dick out and Wendy wraps her legs around my waist as I slide in.

Once, twice and I pull out.

"No!" Wendy cries with dismay.

I grin and kiss her again, kiss her deeply, my tongue exploring her mouth. I move my mouth to her neck, trailing kisses over her collarbone.

"I'm going to need a condom," I whisper.

"I put one in your pocket," Wendy says breathlessly, her hands gripping my shoulders.

"Seriously?" I check the pocket in my shorts and sure enough, there is the little square foil wrapper. "Aren't you a tricky one?"

"I've decided when I want something I'm going to go get it."

"And is this what you want?" My hands cup her breasts and I trail my tongue to her nipple. I give it a lick with my tongue, a little nip with my teeth and begin to suck it hungrily.

"Oh, god, yes!" she cries. She grasps the back of my head.

Never before have I been with a woman so into me and while part of me – the very hard part of me currently confined to my bathing suit – wants to just fuck her, fuck her as hard as I can because I know that's what she wants. But the other part of me wants to wait and make sure she's enjoying it as much as I am.

Deep down, I want to see if I can make her beg for it.

I move my mouth away. "Stop," Wendy moans. "You're a tease."

"You have no idea," I grin. Then I spread her legs right there on the counter, pulling one up so that her foot is resting on the edge and she has to lean back to keep her balance.

Her pussy is wide open to me. I put my hand between her legs, cupping her, feeling her heat, but not doing much else. I lean in and kiss her, keeping my hand firmly in place until she presses her hips forward, presses her pussy against my hand. She gives a little whimpering moan.

"Do you want me to do something here?" I ask as innocently as I can, moving my mouth to her neck, kissing my way to behind her ear and then down to the depth of her cleavage, using my lips and tongue, never touching her breast and never moving my hand.

"Nathan—please!" she finally cries, her voice loud in the quiet house.

"What?"

"Goddamn it!"

I chuckle at the sound of desperation in her voice, feeling a rush of power. This woman *wants* me. She wants me to fuck her senseless.

And there's nothing I want more than to oblige her.

I watch her face as my thumb finds her clit, and my fingers slide inside her. So warm and wet—I thrust my fingers in, searching for the elusive G-spot.

Almost immediately Wendy gasps and she arches forward so much I'm afraid she's going to fall off the counter.

"Did you—?" I ask with amazement.

"I'm quick," she says grimly. "But don't think you're finished yet."

"No way," I tell her, replacing my hand with my mouth.

I've only tongued two women in my life—Jacey, and a girlfriend in my youth. I've tried so many times with Emma, convinced she'll enjoy it if only she'll relax enough, but she never lets me. I was never sure of my technique, but Jacey seemed to enjoy it quite a bit when we were together at Tia's, so I feel confident enough to give it a try with Wendy.

I use firm strokes of my tongue, covering her entire pussy, thrusting inside her before focusing on her tiny little nub; the spot if I rub enough, Emma begins to relax and enjoy things.

It must be the magic spot for Wendy too because she cries out as soon as I circle it with my tongue.

I work up a rhythm – tongue her firmly, circle it slowly and then use my mouth to suck it. The second time I try this, I plunge my fingers inside her as well and I'm rewarded by Wendy crying out and pushing on the back of my head.

"Don't stop!" she gasps.

I smile as I continue. I have no intention of stopping. If only I can get Emma to enjoy this as much...

I hold Wendy steady on the counter with one hand as I work her with the other. Soon – so soon – she's thrusting herself greedily against my mouth, asking – begging – me not to stop, to keep going.

I have no intention of stopping. I continue, licking her quickly, sucking her as hard as I can, thrusting my fingers inside, conscious of how much she's enjoying what I'm doing to her.

I can't even tell she's about to come until she explodes around me with a harsh cry that sounds almost primal.

"Holy shit," she finally gasps as her body stops its convulsions.

I take that as my signal to stop and lift my head. "I can keep going," I offer, grinning at her flushed cheeks, and the glazed expression in her eyes.

Wendy shakes her head. "I need you to fuck me now," she tells me.

"Sounds good to me." I put the condom on as quickly as I can, grasp her ass with both hands and pull her so she's balancing on the very edge. And then using all the willpower I can muster, I slide in nice and slow and steady, even though I really want to fuck her senseless.

Wendy wraps her legs around my waist again. "You stay in there this time," she orders.

"I'm not going anywhere," I tell her, pulling out so only the tip of my cock is inside, then pushing forward to fill completely. I keep my rhythmic pace.

Wendy's eyes are closed and she grips my shoulder with one hand, the other holding the edge of the granite counter. "That feels so good," she breathes, "but I need you to fuck me harder."

"You're so polite," I tell her. "Like this?" I slam against her and she cries out.

"Oh, god yes!"

I'm afraid to do it as hard as I want, afraid I'll hurt her. Her pussy is so wet and warm and it feels so good. Wendy keeps begging me harder, faster, *more*. I unwrap her legs from around my waist and push them against her chest. She has to hold on to the counter with both hands as I fuck her harder, deeper.

The slap of our bodies and Wendy's cries are the only noises in the house.

I groan as she reaches out and grabs my ass. "More," she gasps.

In a quick move, I pull her off the counter and push her so she's lying over it. Grasping her hips with both hands, I fuck her as hard as I can, pumping roughly, with no finesse, no longer concerned with her pleasure because I know this is how she wants it.

"Yes!" she screams and continues screaming and I thrust into her, my legs slapping against hers, lifting her onto her toes with the force. And then her orgasm hits and with a long-drawn-out scream she comes.

Something inside me snaps as all my willpower is gone. Thrusting once, twice, and the third lifting her right off her feet, I come with a lion's roar and empty myself inside her.

When it's over, I slump against her, unable to move.

"Oh, my God," Wendy finally says, rousing me, and I pull out of her. I've never had sex like that before.

"Can I come for another swim next time I'm off?" I ask with a grin.

"You better," she tells me.

Next up is the one you've been waiting for—Interludes III!with Tia, Dominic and Joe!

Interludes III

ANNA ELLIS

THREE BIRDS PRESS

Contents

Tia

"I LIKE YOUR NEW friends," Declan says.

"I thought you might," I tell him with a smile. "Can I assume that's the reason you're back to visit so soon?"

Usually, Declan and Nathalie make the trip from Montreal a few times a year; it had only been seven weeks since they had last visited. Seven weeks since they had met Jacey.

"Of course, we're here to see you," Nathalie assures me with her twinkle. "But it would be a shame not to get to know you're friends a little more while we're here."

I had met the two of them for dinner halfway between their hotel in the city and the school where I am the headmistress. Declan had given business meetings as the main reason they had travelled back from Montreal so soon, but given his fast-approaching retirement, I doubted it. I had seen something in his eye when he had met Jacey at my house and I recognized it as a hunter sensing new prey.

I recognize it because I was once myself that new prey.

"We haven't planned a get-together for this weekend," I tell Declan and Nathalie regretfully. "But Jacey might like it if you dropped in."

"Is she a drop-in type of girl?" Declan wants to know. Nathalie and I share a glance. She understands what her husband is like and whole-heartedly approves because she is the same way. The two of them are sensual, hungry – almost insatiable. I thought long and hard before I allowed them to meet my neighbours on Honeysuckle Court, worried my friends' tentative foray into the world of swinging might forever be tainted by the wild ways of Declan and Nathalie.

These days I realize I should have given them more credit, especially Melissa and the other women. Before Jacey and Dominic had moved in, it had been our former neighbour Molly who was the most eager and open to new experiences and relished the visits from Declan and Nathalie.

Declan was fond of all the women on the street, but it seems Jacey had especially caught his eye, which doesn't surprise me in the least. She seems to catch everyone's eye.

"I think Jacey might be that kind of girl," I say, hiding my smile at the thought of the times Jacey has dropped in on me. The last time had been with Dominic, giving me hope I might have found myself a couple to play with again.

"I'm not sure we'll invite Joe this time," Nathalie muses with a wrinkle of her nose. "He didn't seem as into it as he has been in the past. Have his interests changed? Does he not like Jacey?"

"Quite the opposite, I imagine," I tell them ruefully, shaking my head as the waiter offers me a dessert menu. Declan orders an espresso for him and Nathalie.

"Oh, really?" Nathalie asks in delight. "Has our little Joe found a new friend? It's been a while since Michelle left, but it's a shame this Jacey is married. Or has his interests *really* changed?"

Declan guffaws. "Not my boy, Joe!"

"Has he ever been 'your boy Joe'?" Nathalie presses, toying with her glass of wine. "The two of you have spent an *awful* lot of time together."

We laugh at the thought of Joe as anything other than a raging heterosexual.

"I'm pretty sure Joe hasn't switched teams, no matter how hurt he was when Michelle left."

"You both were," Nathalie reminds me. "I'll never forgive her for that."

"I wasn't married to her," I point out.

"Yes, but your involvement with Joe and Michelle was the most serious relationship you have had since your marriages," Nathalie argues. "Other than us, of course. I often wondered if you had taken things too far. It's easy to do if you're not careful. You had no prescript when you got into a triad with them. You were on equal footing with us—I don't think they ever saw you like that."

"Joe did," I say reluctantly.

"Michelle didn't know the rules," Nathalie complains. "She saw you as disposable—as a unicorn."

"I've never minded that term," I confess as a protest to Nathalie's dismissive tone.

"Trust me, my love, if you've been around as long as we have, you would not want to be referred to as a unicorn. If you enter into a triad, then you need things to be equal. You got involved with Joe and Michelle because you were lonely, and missed us," Nathalie explains. "You could have gotten hurt – emotionally, and for that reason, I worried about it."

"I think you loved Joe and Michelle more than you did your second husband," Declan adds.

"I was a young widow with three small children," I say grimly, remembering that time in my life and still preferring to discuss it rather than Joe and Michelle. "It was better for everyone for me to have a husband. Peter was a good man."

But not the love of my life. He didn't come close to what Marcus meant to me. But he did accept a ready-made family when he met me, and for that, I have to be grateful.

"It's too bad you had to pick such an *unimaginative* one," Nathalie shudders, thankfully moving off the topic of Joe and Michelle and my being a naïve 'unicorn'.

A unicorn is the third person in a triad – a single person sexually involved with a married couple. Usually, there are rules and demands associated with their role, some of which are seen as degrading and unfair, not to mention exploitive, but it had never been like that with Joe and Michelle. True, we didn't have a 'prescript' which is a set of rules for the relationship, but I felt we didn't need one, and Joe didn't know any better.

Joe did whatever Michelle wanted. I'm sure he would have preferred a closed marriage, but Michelle would have never been happy being confined to one person for her entire life.

"Not one of my better choices," I shrug, relieved at Nathalie's short attention span.

"Luckily, he didn't last long," Declan says insensitively, raising his glass of Chateau-Neuf-de-pape to me. "And then we got you back."

"You knew it wouldn't have been forever," I smile fondly at Declan.

Declan had been best friends with my first husband Marcus, inseparable since childhood. When Marcus died, Declan and Nathalie were there to help me pick up the pieces. Declan was godfather to my girls; not that I expected any religious guidance from him. Declan is the most hedonistic, often selfish man I have ever known. I'm still not sure how he remained friends with Marcus. Marcus was stoic, solid and stable and I loved him dearly. The day he died was the worst day of my life.

It was, however, the beginning of my new life.

I had been living in the city at that time. I still remember the night I confessed to Nathalie how much I missed being intimate with someone.

It had been months since Marcus died and the girls had finally returned to their own beds at night. Sleeping four to a bed had been disastrous to all of our sleep habits, but necessary for all of us. But once the girls found they were able to sleep on their own, I found I missed the comfort of having a body in the big bed. After a bottle of wine with Nathalie, I confessed how long it had been since I shared my bed with a man, not to mention my body.

"You don't have to miss it," Nathalie said.

"Can you honestly see me going out and 'hooking up' with someone?" I asked ruefully, using quotations around the word. "I don't even know if that's the proper term anymore. And what about the girls? No," I shook my head. "It would take so long to find someone compatible, and then I would have to get to know them. And I don't want to meet anyone new! I still love Marcus and meeting a new man seems disloyal to him. It's not worth it for a casual fling."

"You should meet another man, but not until you're ready," Nathalie told me.

"Until then, I'll just have to wait," I said sadly.

"No, you don't," she said enigmatically.

I had looked at her with annoyance, a memory I laugh about now. "I'm not the type to pick up a random person, Nathalie. You should know that about me."

"I mean, it doesn't have to be a random person. What if it was someone you know and already care about?"

I must have looked as puzzled as I felt. "I'm not aware of any single men in my social circle," I told her and Nathalie laughed.

"Oh, my love, you really must have a more open mind about this!"

"I don't understand."

"Obviously. What I am trying to do, and failing utterly, is to discretely proposition you."

I didn't understand, not right away. I wasn't the most sophisticated person, but I don't think I was that naïve. I had never considered what Nathalie was offered.

Actually, I hadn't been entirely sure what she had been offering. Luckily, she knew me well enough to realize she had teased me enough and got down to the business of explaining.

"At times, Declan and I enjoy bringing a third party into the bedroom," she began tactfully.

"Oh. I didn't know that."

"I know you didn't. We didn't think Marcus would approve."

I thought of my husband. He was a good, kind and caring man and made me very happy; in the bedroom and out. But he wouldn't have thought much of his best friend and another woman. *"No, he might not have agreed with that,"* I said carefully.

"And you? Do you think we are nothing more than perverse degenerates?" Nathalie asked with a questioning smile.

"Of course not. But..."

"Tia, I enjoy being with both men and women. Declan enjoys watching, and having someone else to play with. It makes us happy. We've been enjoying this for years and have been thinking of possibly inviting you to be that third party..."

"Oh!"

I took a few weeks to think about Nathalie's proposition. And then it took a few weeks to organize it, to find a time where the three of us could be alone.

I had been with a woman once before, in my twenties. Actually, it had been two women, involving a deserted locker room and the close confinement of a sauna. It remained one of the most exciting sexual experiences of *my life, but after that one time, I had never gotten another opportunity to explore that side of me. I had been satisfied by Marcus but a woman's body had always been a source of mystery and wonder to me.*

Nathalie was no exception.

Nathalie wasn't a classically beautiful woman but to me, she was one of the sexiest women I'd ever seen. She was a few years older and clearly experienced in this lifestyle, so I thought she would be the perfect person for me to be with.

I never once gave a second thought to whether stepping over this line would somehow damage our friendship. I was confident it would only bring us closer together. Luckily, I was right.

The night it finally happened, I went to their house. After a few glasses of wine, Nathalie took me by the hand to their bedroom upstairs and undressed me before helping me lay down in the middle of their huge bed.

And then she touched me with fingers and mouth, knowing exactly how gentle and how firm a touch I wanted; knowing what I wanted an instant before I did. She brought me to orgasm so easily while Declan watched, then again while Declan had sex with her. And then I brought her to orgasm while Declan had sex with me.

The night completely overshadowed the incident in the sauna with the two women, and I eagerly became their frequent playmate after that. I was sexually satisfied without the burden of opening my heart to another man. It was the perfect solution.

"Where did you go?" Nathalie wonders, bringing me back to the present. "Did we lose you?"

"I was thinking about our first time," I confess.

"Ah," Declan smiles at me. "Fond memories." He leans over to me and rubs his hand against the back of my neck, pulling me close enough to drop a kiss on the side of my head.

"You were really quite wonderful that night," Nathalie says with an affectionate smile. She reaches out among the clutter of the table and takes my hand.

"Shall we come back to the house with you?" Declan asked eagerly.

"I would like nothing better, but unfortunately not tonight, no." I shook my head ruefully. "All three girls are home tonight and I would like to keep my private actions private."

Nathalie shook her finger at her husband. "Greedy, greedy. We've already planned on dropping by to see Jacey while we are here; can you not wait? Not that it wouldn't be wonderful to see you again," she added. "It has been a while."

"Too long," I say. "But you seem to want to get paired up with my friends..."

"Yes, well, if you have a chance for a little variety..." Declan chuckles. "I think we can all agree that's important to us all."

Sometimes I wonder how I got here; this place in my life without a serious relationship but instead involved in a polyamory lifestyle with my friends and neighbours. I was responsible for introducing a group of people to open marriages and swinging. It has been beneficial for everyone...so far.

What happens when someone takes things too far? What will happen if emotions get in the way?

"Tell me about Joe and Jacey," Nathalie urges, once again pulling me out of my pessimistic reverie.

"I really don't know much," I confess. "Joe hasn't spoken to me about her. It's only what I've seen."

"And what have you seen?" Declan prompts eagerly.

I smiled teasingly at him. "Nothing that would interest you. I've only seen how Joe looks at her. But Jacey is married and happy. Dominic is really quite wonderful."

"Tell us how you really feel about him," Nathalie teases.

To my dismay, I feel my cheeks redden. "It's not like that."

"Oh, no? I saw how you looked at him that night. I don't blame you. I was tempted myself."

I don't like how the thought of Nathalie with Dominic pains my heart.

"You've never minded sharing," Declan adds. "Neither has Joe. Do you think Jacey will finally help him get over Michelle?"

"I'm not sure if he ever will get over her," Nathalie muses. "If the two of you didn't work out, I can't see him trying with anyone. That woman had some sort of mysterious hold over him. And you. I have never understood it."

After dinner, I say goodbye and head home by myself. I've never minded being alone, being the third wheel. In fact, I would have preferred to remain unmarried after Marcus' death, but it had proven difficult with three young girls. April had been four when her father died, and the twins were almost two. I met Peter five years after Marcus died, and he was sweet and unassuming and loved the idea of having three daughters as well as a wife.

When I married Peter, I gained a partner and some help with the day-to-day challenges of raising the girls, but doing so meant I had to sacrifice my relationship with Nathalie and Declan. Peter had no idea about that side of my life, but I knew he wouldn't want to share me with them. He wasn't that type of man.

Unfortunately, we were only a family for a short time. Peter died in a car crash two years after we had married.

That was when I moved the girls to Honeysuckle Court for a fresh start.

When I got home, I checked on them and found all three girls sweetly asleep in their beds. April was almost fifteen now, the twins twelve. They were the main babysitters of my friends' children so I could have no issue with them staying at home alone. But I did like it when the four of us were home together.

Other than the years with Marcus, I've been the happiest here on Honeysuckle Court. The girls quickly adjusted,, I love being the head-mistress of my school and I've met such good friends.

I met Joe and Michelle soon after moving onto the street. Melissa and Mahak were already living here, and Molly and Jason were in the house Jacey and Dominic lived in now. It took a while for me to get to know them, and Wendy and Jackson, who moved in soon after. Paige and Colin came a year after them. But in the beginning, there were only Joe and Michelle.

Michelle was a wild one. There was nothing she wouldn't or had al-ready done. I had met them at one of Declan and Nathalie's parties, one of the last they held before they moved to Montreal.

I got the idea of the key parties from them.

Michelle and I had enjoyed each other's company that evening and for several other evenings after that, with and without Joe. The two of them seemed to have an open marriage, albeit one-sided. Michelle had explained early on how she found it impossible to be monogamous, and if Joe wanted to be with her, he had to accept that. Obviously, he did, since they had been married for almost ten years, and had a little boy, Finn.

Once Declan and Nathalie moved to Montreal, I introduced the idea of becoming a triad with Michelle and Joe. That was the main reason they moved to the street behind Honeysuckle Court.

I spent quite a few years with the two of them. Michelle and I benefitted most from the sexual side of the relationship, but I quickly found myself drawn to Joe. He reminded me a lot of Marcus; quiet and serious but with a great sense of humour. He is a good, decent man. And amazing in bed.

Joe and I became friends, much closer than Michelle and I. I didn't have much in common with Michelle. She was impulsive, brash and opinion-ated and could be downright unlikable at times. But she was also funny, big-hearted and loyal. Plus, she knew exactly what my body needed. But it was with Joe that I found the confidant I needed, a true friend. We could talk about everything and anything. He became the man in my life, my daughters' lives; a role model of what a decent man should be. Joe would help me around the house. Michelle was often away with work and Joe would bring Finn over to share dinner with the girls and I. The kids would play, or we'd help them with their homework; Joe and I would talk as we made dinner together.

When Michelle wasn't there, it was like we were a family. I tried not to feel the pang when he returned home, or when I didn't see him for a while. He wasn't my husband, I would remind myself. I was only borrowing him from Michelle – sharing him.

I told myself that was enough.

I'm thinking about the last time I had been with Michelle when I got into bed later that night.

I realized I was bisexual when Nathalie explained it to me. It helped with the confusion I often felt growing up – having crushes on both boys and girls, neither of which I would talk about. Michelle made no bones about ignoring her sexuality. Before Joe, she had lived with a woman. Michelle was open and free, opinionated and passionate about anything and everything.

The last night I had been with them, Michelle had opened the door to me, clad only in a towel.

"Joe's dropping off Finn at his mother's for his sleepover," Michelle informed me. "Come on upstairs."

Normally, we would have waited for Joe. Michelle would pour us an overflowing glass of wine while we chatted. Despite our differences, Michelle had become one of my best friends along with my lover.

I didn't ask about Joe as I followed Michelle upstairs. I shut the bedroom door behind us as Michelle flopped on the bed. I began to unbutton my shirt. She seemed as eager to begin as I was.

"I want to you use this on me first," she instructed, holding up a smooth purple vibrator. "I'm so unbelievably horny right now and I can't wait. Then I can play with you for longer."

Like me, Michelle loved to give pleasure but she teased and taunted and liked to make me beg.

I shed my clothes quickly and Michelle threw the vibrator at me. The buzz filled the room as I turned it on. "You're impatient," I teased.

She rolled her eyes as I lay on the bed beside her. "Joe hasn't touched me in three days. He's all worried about this big job he has due and I've been reading those new Fifty Shade books and they get me so turned on. I used the shower head yesterday."

"I haven't read them yet."

"You have to. Writing sucks except for the sex parts but she comes up with stuff even I've never tried. Not that I've ever really been into BDSM."

"Something you haven't tried?" I laughed.

"Not much I haven't," she agreed.

I ran my hand up her leg. Michelle was curvy and voluptuous and I envied her curves. I leaned over and kissed her as I pressed the vibrator between her legs. We had been together so much that I knew her body by touch. I knew I had the right spot when she moaned against my mouth.

Michelle's hands found my breasts as I slipped the vibrator inside her. Her breathing had already quickened as I thrust the vibrator in and out before touching it to her clit.

"There," she groaned, throwing her head back against the pillows. "Theretherethere—don't stop."

I twirled the vibrator around the sensitive nub, thumbing the switch to adjust the speed. Michelle had already begun thrusting her hips toward me and I knew it wouldn't take her long. I felt the anticipation between my legs at the thought of my turn.

"Oh, my God, Tia!" Michelle cried out. She grasped one of her breasts and began toying with her nipple. I leaned over and flicked the other one *with my tongue as I increased the vibrations even more. Michelle needed clitoral stimulation for her orgasms, so I concentrated on that.*

"Oh, yes!" Michelle cried out loudly as her body stiffened. "Oh, my god," *she added after she relaxed from the orgasm. "I needed that. And now I* *need you."*

Taking no time to recover, Michelle soon had me on my hands and knees *near the end of the bed.*

"Your ass looks so good like that," she complimented me. My head rested *on my arms with my bottom in the air. She gave my cheek a teasing slap.* *"Maybe I could learn something from that book," she mused.*

I didn't reply. Michelle knew there wasn't much I wouldn't try. My *sexual appetite had increased exponentially over the years, as I learned* *more about what my body wanted and giving in to its demands.*

Michelle slapped me again, a little harder this time and I jerked from *the sting. "Like that?" she asked, slipping two fingers inside me "Yes, you* *did. You're so wet. Maybe you liked making me come. Is that it?" She thrust* *her fingers in and out as she spoke.*

"Yes," I told her in a low voice.

"You like me more than Joe, don't you?"

I couldn't answer that. I loved being with both of them but would never *be able to choose between them.*

Michelle thrust harder when I refused to answer, and then suddenly *pulled out her fingers. "'Cause I can make you wait for him. I can play* *with myself and leave you for him. Is that what you want?"*

Despite not being into BDSM, Michelle was more dominant than she *realized.*

"No," I told her.

"You're such a dirty girl," she continued, plunging her fingers back inside *me. I could feel her breath against my sensitive skin as she leaned down.* *"Always so classy, almost prissy on the outside, but look at you with your ass*

in the air, just begging me to tongue you. Is that what you want? You want me to use my tongue – here?" She pressed her tongue against my clitoris.

"Yes. Please," I said breathlessly.

"And here?" She replaced her fingers with her tongue, probing in and out roughly.

"Yes," I gasped.

"And here?" Drawing her tongue out, she licked along my cleft to my anus and pushed her tongue against the puckered skin.

"Yes." I couldn't help myself and push back against her. I felt her chuckle.

"You're so dirty. That's why I love you so much."

That was the last she spoke. Her fingers returned inside me, thrusting furiously as she leaned down so that her head was almost hanging underneath me and began tonguing me, licking my clitoris with absolutely no finesse, but in a way that was almost unbearably exciting for me.

I would soon learn after I met Mahak, what a master in cunnilingus was like. But until that occurred, I enjoyed Michelle's assault on me.

Licking and sucking, probing and thrusting. Her fingers were everywhere – inside my vagina, in my anus, stroking my clitoris. Her tongue was just as busy.

"Lay down on your back," she suddenly instructed, taking away her fingers with no notice.

I obeyed quickly, but Michelle paused before resuming. "If anyone could see you now," she mocked. "Ready to beg for it. Ready to beg for this," she added, running her fingers along my breasts. "When was the first time you were with a woman? Not Nathalie. There had to be someone before her."

"I told you about the time in the sauna," I said, wanting her touch but not willing to beg for it. Yet.

"Tell me again," she asked.

I closed my eyes as Michelle trailed her fingers down to my inner thigh, coming closer to where I longed to be touched, but never close enough. "It *was years ago; I had been working out in the gym one night. It was quiet, hardly anyone had been there."*

"What happened when you went into the change room?" Michelle asked eagerly.

"I liked to sit in the sauna so I took off all my clothes and opened the door. But I didn't realize there were two women in there already."

"What were they doing?" Michelle continued to stroke my thighs, and my belly.

"It was a big sauna, with two levels of benches. One of the women was sitting on the top level, the other kneeling on the seat below. She had her head between the woman's legs."

"What was she doing?"

"She was—oral sex," I stammered. Despite my openness when it came to the act, I still had difficulty describing things. I preferred not to use the more vulgar words and terms, and Michelle knew this. She liked pushing me to say the words I normally couldn't.

"But what was she doing?" Michelle insisted. She leaned over me and pressed her mouth between my legs once more. I couldn't stop the soft moan that escaped when she touched me and spread my legs wider. "Did she use her mouth?"

"Her tongue," I said, inwardly begging Michelle to do the same.

"Like this?" I pressed my hips upward as she demonstrated.

"Yes. Oh!"

"Then what happened?" Michelle asked, pausing with her mouth so close to my clitoris I could feel her breath.

"They saw me standing there. I couldn't move – I stood and watched them."

"You were excited."

"Yes."

"Like now. You're so excited now." Michelle licked my cleft, quickly and I gasped. "What did they do?"

"*They—they smiled and when I started to apologize they invited me in. And then they both started touching me. They made me lay down on the bench, and one touched my breasts and the other...the other...*"

"*What did she do?*" Michelle demanded in a low voice. "*Tell me what she did to you.*"

"*She used her mouth...her tongue. She licked me...there...*"

"*Your pussy,*" Michelle mocked, moving her fingers back inside me. "*Say it with me.*"

"*Pussy,*" I gasped.

"*Good girl. She went down on you. She ate your pussy. She did what you love me to do.*"

"*Yes!*"

"*You want me to do that again. You want me to lick your pussy?*"

"*Yes. Oh —yes!*" Michelle's fingers were thrusting relentlessly inside me, her thumb rubbing my clitoris roughly. She had a wicked grin on her face, enjoying my discomfort.

"*Say please.*" She knelt on the bed between my legs, pulling at my hips to bring them closer.

"*Please,*" I gasped as her tongue once again began to probe me. She spread my lips with her fingers, opening me wide as she began to lash me with her tongue. "*Oh, please!*"

Michelle assaulted my clitoris relentlessly, licking and sucking until tremors raced up and down my body and I didn't recognize my voice making the noises in the room.

And then the door opened.

"*You didn't wait for me?*" Joe asked.

I looked at him with surprise. He was staring at Michelle, at what she was doing to me, without a hint of an expression on his face.

"*Come and fuck me, big boy,*" Michelle told him, wrenching her mouth away from me, but continuing with her fingers. "*You know you want to.*"

Joe was a quiet man, but even more so in the bedroom. I watched as he pulled down his pants and thrust into his wife from behind.

Nothing got Michelle as excited as when we were in this position.

Now, her moans and cries filled the room, muffled as her mouth returned to giving me pleasure. I closed my eyes as I began to feel the stirrings deep inside me.

"Yes!" Michelle cried sharply. "Fuck me just like that, Joe. Just like that."

I chanced another glance and met Joe's eyes. He was staring straight at me, still with absolutely no expression on his face as he thrust into his wife. I held his gaze for as long as I could but had difficulty concentrating as my orgasm drew closer. Sensations ran up my arms and legs, gathering in my core until I exploded with a sharp cry.

Almost in unison, Michelle came as well.

"Enough," she cried as soon as she was able to speak. "Joe, with Tia now. I want to watch."

"What?" he demanded.

Nodding her head, Michelle pulled away from him and crawled along the bed to the nightstand where they kept a box of condoms. "Here," she instructed again, quickly rolling the prophylactic onto his cock. "Fuck her. I want to watch."

Joe had no choice. I waited as he crawled onto the bed. "Okay?" he asked me, as he slid into me.

"Of course," I held my breath as he began to move within. Joe was well-endowed and knew how to use it. Sex with him always reminded me why I preferred both ways.

Joe propped himself on his arms and thrust into me, thankfully starting slowly because I was still sensitive from my first orgasm. Gradually my body began to respond to him, faster and harder, egged on by Michelle on the bed beside us.

"Harder. Fuck her hard, Joe. You know she likes it like that. She likes it hard and fast – she likes it dirty."

It wasn't often that I had someone watch as I had sex, and it excited me more than I expected it to. But then I tuned out Michelle. I wasn't listening to her. As Joe thrust into me, my body rocking to meet his, it was only him and I together on the bed. His strong body pressed against me, his hands pulling up my legs, his hands on my breasts, in my hair, drawing me even closer to him.

His mouth against mine.

It was the kiss that did it for me. Joe kissed me as he made love to me and it was like I had never been with a man before. It was so intimate, so secret, regardless of Michelle being there with us.

I began to feel the familiar sensations once again race along my body but for once I didn't want it to end. Having Joe pressed against me, moving inside me... "Oh, my God!" I finally cried, unable to bear the pleasure any longer. "Joe!"

And I exploded around him once again. Almost immediately, his body stiffened and with barely a sound, he emptied into me. When he rested his weight on me, my hands somehow became tangled with his. We stayed that way, hands entwined, bodies resting together until Michelle spoke.

Thinking of Michelle, thinking of that night always excites me. But I always stop remembering there.

I think about how it felt to be in Joe's arms, how nice it was to have a man hold me, to make love to me, rather than just sex. Because that's what it had been with Joe. We made love for the first time that night. It may have begun as a scene with Michelle, Joe and I but it finished with Joe and I making love.

Before I climbed under the covers, I got my tiny vibrator from my drawer and I turned it on as I thought about how it had been with Joe. And Michelle. No woman had ever touched me like she did. Other than Nathalie, she had been the only one I had ever let take control of my body like that.

I touched the vibrator between my legs, remembering the feel of Michelle's fingers, her tongue in the same spot. As I rubbed it along my cleft, moving it around my clitoris in slow circles, I shut my mind to that night, about what happened next. I recalled her mouth, her fingers, the sensations she evoked in my body...

The feeling of Joe's body on mine, his hips thrusting against mine, my hands clasped in his...

Head thrown back against the pillows, eyes closed, I remembered his body against mine, moving inside me, thrusting urgently, his face against my neck, my breasts...

With a soft sigh, I climax, feeling the release of my body as I sink into the bed, my body lax and spent. Only then do I permit myself to remember...

"You liked it better with him!" Michelle accused as Joe rolled off me.

I was bewildered by her accusation. I was still reeling from my orgasms, by the realization it had never been like that with Joe and me before.

What had begun as fun playtime with Michelle and me ended with Joe making love to me as she watched. And from the sounds of it, she didn't approve.

"I—" I stammered. "I like it with you, too!"

"But it was better with him," she accused.

"I'm not saying that. I'm not saying anything!"

"Michelle," Joe warned, but she continued.

"Look at you! You don't look like that after I fuck you."

"You told me to," Joe said.

"That wasn't fucking, you made love to her!"

I couldn't say anything because that was how I had felt too. I refused to look at Joe.

"It's the same thing," Joe tried but lacked any conviction in his voice. That was when I knew I was right, Michelle was right.

"It is not! This is about sex and fucking and having fun – not love! The only one you should be making love to is me!"

"I'm going to go now," I said, hastily gathering my clothes.

"Probably a good idea," Joe said in a low voice, as Michelle continued to scream obscenities at him.

Once I had dressed, I chanced a look at Joe. He had pulled his pants on and was standing with his eyes on the floor, not responding to any of Michelle's accusations.

And there were quite a few of them.

"Do you make love with Nathalie too?"

"Has there been anyone else?"

"What is it about her?"

"Are you in love with her?"

I left after that, escaping the room with my tail between my legs, feeling horribly guilty for leaving Joe to fend for myself but there was nothing I could do. Michelle was out of control.

Michelle left Joe that night, taking her things, as well as their son Finn's, and moved out.

I never once spoke to Joe about what happened that night.

Dominic

I HEAD FOR THE staff room during my prep period. It's unusually quiet today with only two other teachers. No Emma, which is probably a good thing because when she's around I chat with her rather than getting anything finished. I have a bunch of papers I need to get marked today so I don't have to do them tonight.

Tonight Jacey is taking me out to dinner for my birthday.

At least I think she is. She hasn't exactly told me what she has planned. I can't imagine her coming up with any other suggestions. For someone with an almost-genius I.Q., Jacey isn't that imaginative when it comes to romantic options for celebrating.

She's getting pretty good when it comes to dreaming up sexual scenarios, however.

I'm immersed in red, marking the most disastrous essay comparing King Lear to Ned Stark of *Game of Thrones* when my cell makes the weird sci-fi sound that Hanna selected for my text signal.

I don't recognize the number and there's no message, only a picture.

I zoom in with my fingers. It's Jacey. She hates having her picture taken and refuses to participate in the selfie fad. She even hates Facebook.

I think this is a selfie – the picture is Jacey is standing in our bedroom wearing nothing but a smile.

I think she's holding a sign but I can't stop staring at her breasts to focus on the paper she's holding in front of her belly.

"What the..." I mutter aloud.

The sign says Happy Birthday! I think she must have used Hanna's crayons to write it, not that I'd care if she smeared ketchup and mustard on a card. The sight of my naked wife in the middle of the day is an unexpected treat. But for her to send me a naked selfie at work...she must be up to something. I spend a few minutes admiring the picture before I respond to her, glad the staff room is empty for once.

Thx, I finally texted back with a happy face. The one showing the big smile.

Hoping it brightens your day.

I scroll to find the emoji for the sun and send it to my wife. *Definitely.*

I try to return to the essay, but can't stop smiling for the longest time. Unfortunately, it slowly fades as I continue reading the slop of an essay. It's something about how both Lear and Ned Stark as kings had been fatally betrayed by those they loved best, especially their daughters...

Is this kid an idiot? Sure, it's a good premise, but all of my students know I'm a huge *Game of Thrones* fan, so if they're that much of a brown-noser to include the characters in an essay, they should damn well get the characters straight.

My cell whistles again.

Another picture. What are you up to, Jacey? I wonder.

But this isn't my wife. It's Wendy, Jackson's wife. And *she's* naked.

Why is Wendy sending me naked pictures of herself?

Not that I don't appreciate it.

Wendy is tall and slim, still with a hint of the muscular swimmer's shoulders. I didn't know she was a swimmer until a few weeks ago when I saw her dive into her new pool.

That was the night I also watched her and Jacey play in the water together as Wendy sucked my cock. It had been a good night, a very good night. I'm surprised I remember Wendy telling us she was once on the swim team. The events unrelated to our foursome are a bit hazy.

The fact that the picture shows Wendy standing in her pool, the water reaching mid-thigh, brings the events of the night all back. I like to think of myself as adventurous – God knows I have to be with Jacey – but never before have I been involved in a foursome.

It makes me look at Wendy in a whole new light.

Her blonde hair is loose and hangs to her shoulders. Guessing from the way her breasts are tight and how erect her nipples are, I deduce the water must be cold. She has an inflatable swim ring around her waist, with the duck's head upside down and the bill tucked between her legs.

What the hell?

Lucky ducky, I text back. Two can play this game, although I'm still in the dark about what game they are playing. Will there be more pictures? Maybe some with the two of them?

I reluctantly go back to the essay, keeping one eye on my phone. Lear's descent into madness is mirrored by Stark's son Joffrey. This kid has clearly never watched the show.

Another whistle. I snatch up my phone. Another picture.

This time it's Paige. She's posed with her back to the camera, peering over her shoulder, long dark blonde hair pushed out of her eyes and with a big smile on her face. It no longer surprises me that she's naked, with the side of her breast visible from her pose. I'm sure she's trying to be sexy with her hands on her hips like that, but her expression is too cheerful for that. It makes me smile to see her.

The sight of that ass makes me smile as well.

Paige is curvy and rounded and maybe about twenty pounds over-weight but I would never suggest she diet or exercise or do anything for fear of losing the most awesome ass I've ever seen on a mortal woman. It's a perfect heart shape, her cheeks rounded and smooth, the ideal size to be grabbed without having too much booty

Jacey told me Colin is an ass-man and I'm not surprised if that is what he has at home.

You're looking a little cheeky, I text to her. I don't recognize the cell number, so I'm not sure who I'm responding too. Not that it matters – the girls must be together and clearly having fun with me.

I don't even bother returning back to the essay. I'm going to fail him, anyway.

A fourth whistle and I snatch up my phone to see my next present.

My eyes almost pop out of my head with this one.

It's Emma, wearing nothing but a shy smile and giving the camera a little wave.

Out of all of them, she looks the most awkward, and it's the most endearing. I'm not sure what Jacey had to do to convince Emma to take part in this.

I wonder what Jacey had to do to get all of them involved. The thought makes me uncomfortably hard and I shift in my chair. I've still got a full period left before I can get home to question my wife about this.

What a nice present! I text back.

It's a sweet picture of Emma. She's very pretty in a delicate way, which is surprising considering how much of a disciplinarian she is in the classroom. I've witnessed first-hand her tearing into a class.

I cup my hand around my phone in case anyone comes in the staff room, sure Emma would be mortified if anyone but me were to see this. I'm sure Emma will be mortified with *me* seeing this. I spend time with her at work, and Jacey and I have gotten together for drinks with Emma and Nathan, but that's all. And never in our staffroom chats about our students, has Emma ever made mention of the relationship we both share with our neighbours. They have only come to one of Tia's parties and Emma was with Mahak that night.

I've expressed my concerns about how the two facets of my relationship with Emma will co-exist with Jacey. I'm friendly with the other wives and enjoy their company in and out of the bedroom (and the pool, in the case of Wendy) but I don't share the same workplace with them as I do Emma.

"People have office affairs all the time," Jacey pointed out to me when we discussed it. "They can still be professional."

"I think what we have is a little different than an office affair," I protested.

"Not really. You're engaging in an extra-marital affair with someone you work with. Or you will be, once Tia picks her for you, which I'm sure she will soon. If you're both mature enough to handle the swinging with the neighbours thing, then you'll be able to handle continuing to be professional at work. Unless you go and fuck her in a classroom. Have you ever done that with someone?"

That's my wife.

What do I think about her take on our relationship with the neighbours?

It's a difficult question to answer.

I've always known from the beginning Jacey is a very sexual, very adventurous woman. I found myself in bed with her hours after first meeting her years ago in Japan, despite a girlfriend I was very much in love with back home in Toronto. But there was something about Jacey I just couldn't resist. It was like she was some kind of drug. After the night in Japan, I assumed I'd never see her again, but I still couldn't get her out of my mind. And it hadn't been just the sex—although being with Jacey was like nothing I'd ever experienced before.

The list of women I had been with wasn't that long, but long enough to impress on me how no other woman enjoyed sex like Jacey did. She embraces the act like it was her right to get pleasure from it, never using it as a weapon, never seeing the point of refusing. I still think sex is Jacey's favourite thing in life.

So it never surprised me how much Jacey has embraced our new lifestyle. What did surprise me was how long she remained faithful to me in our marriage.

We had talked about our past and so I knew Jacey had never been able to remain monogamous in her previous relationships. In fact, because of this, none of her boyfriends before me had been long-term and she had been extremely anti-marriage at the beginning. I'm sure it was only the one-two punch of her unexpected pregnancy and her mother's passing that got us to the altar. The only thing Jacey's mother wanted for her was to be married before she died so Jacey proposed to me. If it wasn't for that, I doubt we would have ever gotten married.

I wonder if we'd still be together.

I have no doubt that Jacey loves me and we are happy together. But Jacey is a free-spirit and the confines of an institution such as marriage weighs on her. She's done well in the years we've been together. There had only been one misstep that I know of—her fling with my friend Seth, with neither of them aware that I knew about it—but in Jacey's defence, it had taken place during the period of horrible post-partum depression that had me doubting Jacey would ever be able to recover from.

This relationship we've stumbled into with our neighbours is perfect for Jacey. She gets to indulge in all her fantasies with other men (and I know she has a lot of fantasies) and I get to keep my wife. And luckily, I'm the sort of man who is confident enough not to get jealous. It also helps that I'm the type of man who enjoys hearing about her escapades.

And even watching.

My cell whistles again, bringing me out of my reverie about Jacey sleeping with other men. And women. If this keeps up, I'm going to be incapable of teaching my next class.

A fifth text. This one is a picture of Melissa. She's lying on her back, in the middle of their living room floor, naked like the others. Her breasts defy gravity like those only enhanced with implants can do.

I've never seen a woman with a better body than Melissa. Her stomach is tight with abdominal muscles clearly visible and arms that beg to wear tank tops. Melissa is cute as well...my focus drifts down her body where her hand is strategically placed on her hip. Her legs are closed and the area where her legs meet is bare.

She's shaved. That's new.

This is a new side of you, I text.

I put my head in my hands, praying no one comes in the room. I've lost all interest in grading inane essays and can only think about how I'm supposed to get rid of this huge hard-on before class begins.

"No more," I groan aloud as my cell whistles again.

This one is a video rather than a straight picture, and I'm surprised to see Tia sitting on the couch in her living room, as naked as the other women had been. I'm very surprised to see Tia taking part in this, but not unhappy about it. Tia is a beautiful woman; her grace and class mix with her sensuality to make her an enigma any man or woman would love to unravel.

I look up to make sure the other teachers in the room aren't paying attention to me before I push the play button on my cell and watch Tia come to life.

"Hello, Dominic. I hope this little present from us to you has helped make your birthday that much better." She smiles at whoever is recording her, and in a move that would make Sharon Stone proud, does the uncross/cross leg move. My heart practically stops.

"I do hope you're watching this somewhere private," Tia continues with a smile. "We wouldn't want anyone to see this. And of course, it goes without saying—please delete when you're finished watching. I'm sure there will be an encore production sometime in the future."

As I watch, Jacey, Paige, Wendy, Melissa and Emma jump into the video with Tia and give a loud cheer. There is kissing, touching, bare breasts everywhere...everything a man would love to see, especially on his birthday. The only thing missing is a pillow fight.

The finale, after a few minutes of watching the delicious torture, is the six of them with their bare bodies mashed together.

"Happy birthday, Dominic," they shout, each with a big smile on their face.

"Your present," Jacey adds, once the female voices fall silent, "is that you get to pick one of us for tonight. Or two. Your choice."

"That's mean," I say aloud. And to reiterate my point, I text that to them.

All I get in return is a smiley face.

I'm still not sure who it is I'm corresponding with. It's not Jacey's cell number, and I don't know the phone numbers of the others. I wouldn't put it past Jacey to get a throwaway phone for her little game.

How am I supposed to pick one of them?

And who was recording them?

I've been with all of them except for Emma, and while I would love to pick her, it's back to the uncertainty of combining business and pleasure. As for the others, there's something special about each of them...

There's no way I can pick. If Jacey is behind this, it's not fair to make me choose. But I don't know if it is Jacey. I don't want to pick.

You, I text.

Let's see what she does with that.

I make it through my last period with difficulty.

The house is quiet when I finally get home. I remove my key from the door with a sense of disappointment. I hoped Jacey or *someone* would have met me at the door but no one was there.

"Jacey?" I call. No Jacey.

No Ben or Hanna, either and the car is parked out front, so Jacey hasn't gone to pick them up.

At the bottom of the stairs, I see a note.

Happy birthday Dominic!

Please go to the bedroom so you can see who your present is.

Or not see.

Underneath the printed piece of paper is a blindfold.

Don't worry, you'll get dinner later too!

I can't help the shit-eating grin that creases my face. If this is Jacey, she's definitely stepped up her game. If it isn't...

Dutifully, I head upstairs, stopping at the closed bedroom door to tie the blindfold around my head. "Hello?" I call as I enter my bedroom.

Silence. I stand at the door for a few moments, getting used to being in darkness. There's a tiny crack of light under the fabric of the tie but that's it. Soon, my other senses take over.

I hear a movement and feel a hand take my arm, leading me over to the bed. "Jacey?"

Silence. "Are you not talking to me?" I ask teasingly. "I liked the pictures." Still nothing. "Ok, so this is how you want it. Got it. Quiet. Ow."

She leads me to the end of the bed and then gives me a push forward, so I tumble down onto it.

Hands help me turn over on my back. I breathe deeply as my tie is taken off, and my shirt unbuttoned. This doesn't smell like Jacey.

My arms are pulled up and I can feel ties binding me to the headboard. "This is new," I say conversationally. I've tied Jacey up before, but it's never been reciprocated. It's never been something I've wanted to try. But now, here I am lying in bed, arms bound, eyes covered...obviously, this girl is on a mission.

I'm still not certain it's Jacey, though. I'm not sure how I feel about it if it's not.

On one hand, it's exciting to think another woman is setting this stage up for me, presumably with Jacey's blessing. "Is there anyone else here?" I ask, straining my ears for any sounds to indicate if we're alone.

My iPod on my nightstand is turned on in response, masking any sounds I'm listening for. I have no idea if there is a line of people in here with me, watching this.

My belt is undone and slides through the loops with a *snap*.

"Not sure about that," I say nervously, as the leather hits a palm. "Not that I have much of a choice, I guess."

My pants are pulled down roughly and then my underwear. The uncertainty of the situation, and not knowing what's going on has acted as a deterrent to getting hard. Hopefully, I'll be able to rise to the occasion soon. "Well, now. We are definitely getting some—"

My words are cut off as my still-embarrassingly flaccid cock is lifted and taken into a warm mouth.

"—where," I finished weakly.

I harden immediately, caught in the warm wetness. A gentle sucking, a light flickering of the tongue –

This isn't Jacey's style. My hands are bound so I can't touch. All I need to feel is her face, or her hair, or her body.

I would hope I would be able to tell my wife by the feel of her body.

I force myself to relax as her mouth moves up and down my cock, slowly, languidly, like she's playing with me. Which she most certainly is. She tongues the tip with little flickering licks, holding the base of my shaft in her hand and licking like it's an ice cream cone, then stroking the whole cock with her tongue. She cups my balls with one hand.

This is amazing.

The bed shifts as the mystery lady moves and I get the sense she's kneeling beside me, crouched over my cock. I'm just about to make some pithy remark about how comfortable she is when she begins licking her way down my shaft, in between little open-mouth kisses.

And then she begins licking my balls.

"Oh...yeah..." I breathe.

With one firm hand gripping the base of my cock, the other gently cupping my sack, she spends long moments, kissing, and caressing before taking one of my balls into her mouth.

Jacey has never done that before.

On to the next one. By this time, I can hear my own ragged breathing and anything flaccid about me has long been rectified. She returns her attention to my cock and gets serious about it now. Soon I'm moving my hips in response to her mouth travelling along my cock.

This is really amazing.

"Happy birthday to me," I mutter.

And then she stops. "I'm sorry," I cry. "I'll be quiet. Don't—please don't—"

She's moving again and I can feel the brush of a leg against mine. And then I can feel her straddling me, an instant before something even better surrounds my cock.

"Ah, fuck..." I groan.

My cock is enveloped in her welcoming pussy and all I want to do is grip her hips and thrust up and into her, but my arms are tied. I attempt to move my hips, but she puts a hand on my chest and I get the hint she doesn't want me to move.

I think it's Jacey even though a little scene like this is so not her style. She likes me to take charge, to set the rhythm, to enjoy myself and enjoy her. Jacey has always been up for anything but this dominant side is confusing me.

It feels like Jacey. Is it horrible that I can't instantly recognize my wife's pussy?

She rides me slowly, taking her time once again. I can only lay back and enjoy the ride.

If it was Melissa, she wouldn't be able to be this quiet.

If it was Tia, she would be getting a little kinkier.

If it was Wendy—it could be Wendy, but like Jacey, she's never been one to take charge.

It might be Paige. This could well be Paige. I wouldn't mind it if was Paige. I've had fun with her.

It's definitely not Emma. At least I don't think it is. Maybe it could be.

She's moving faster now, gripping me tightly with her muscles. I can hear her breathing above the music and know she's enjoying herself.

Jacey can never keep quiet, whoever this is, is doing a pretty good job of that.

Faster, and harder, riding me so only the tip stays inside as she drives back down, again and again.

"I need to touch you," I moan, straining against my bindings.

I get the sense she's shaking her head at me.

I'm not going to last much longer. The beautiful blowjob, the warm tightness of her pussy—"I'm going to come soon. I need you—touch yourself. I want you to come too."

She might already be doing that because I feel the brush of her fingers against the base of my cock as she slams down.

She increases the speed even more and I groan aloud, so caught up in the sensations I don't care who is riding me right now. The only thing I do care about is the feel of this pussy, this woman impaling herself on my cock and how very good it feels...

The sound of a whimper puts me over the edge and her pussy contracts like a fist.

"Oh, fuck," I cry. "Oh, my fuck..." I thrust up, regardless of what she wants, once, twice and explode into her. "Oh, fuck, yeah."

"You really need some new dialogue," says a familiar voice.

"I was hoping it was you," I say weakly, blinking in the sudden light as my blindfold is removed.

Jacey smiles down at me. "Happy birthday. Did you like your present?"

"I did. All of them. How did you...?" I shake my head. "Maybe I don't want to know how you got them to do that."

"And I won't tell you," my wife says with a grin. "But it was pretty easy to convince them."

"But whose phone was it?" I want to know. "That threw me. And then, this..."

"You actually didn't know it was me?" she asks with surprise. "I think I'm offended."

"You smell differently. You've never tied me up before –" I pull at the ties so she'll get the hint and let me go, "and you've never taken that long to give me a blowjob."

"I was *playing*," she says shyly, stroking my bare chest, still straddling me.

"I like you playing," I tell her with a grin. "Can we play some more?"

"Right now?" she asks with surprise.

"Maybe give me a minute or two," I concede. "Can you untie me?"

"Can't we leave them on?" she says and leans down to kiss me.

This birthday present is definitely one for the books.

THE NIGHT I FIRST met Michelle, she gave me a blowjob.

It had been at a party of a friend of a friend, some holiday celebration I didn't want to be there for. In fact, I had been attempting to leave early when Michelle caught up with me.

I was on my way back to my truck, head down to avoid shouts of incrimination about leaving early when a woman stopped me. She was tall and curvy with masses of dark hair and the biggest brown eyes I'd ever seen.

"You going?" she asked.

I had no idea who she was.

"Pardon?" I stammered; distracted by the way her creamy skin glowed in the moonlight. The party took place on a farm outside the city and the revelry surrounded a giant bonfire in the middle of a field. I noticed outside the circle of fire that the summer night had cooled.

"Why are you leaving?" she asked. Instead of being annoyed by this, which would have been the case if anyone else had stopped me, I was somewhat amused. Maybe it was how her tone insinuated that she had every right to demand to know my whereabouts.

"Parties aren't really my thing," I told her. I was thirty-one—not old in any way—but old enough to know better than to sit around a fire all night, drinking copious amounts of beer and rye, watching others perform acts of stupidity and depravity and think I could function the next day. Not that I had plans for the next day, but it was nice to know I'd be able to get out of bed if I had to.

"That's good to know," she said, wrapping her arms around her waist.

"Why?" I don't know what made me halt my escape to talk to her, but there was something about her that intrigued me. Plus, I am a man and her breasts were spectacular.

"Because most of those guys are jerks trying to get me drunk so they can get in my pants. They're too stupid to realize all a woman wants is a little attention and then she's wide open for the asking."

"Is that so?" Definitely intriguing. I'd put her age at between twenty-five and thirty. It's difficult to tell for a woman, and even harder to ask. I moved off the path back to let a couple stumble by.

"Look at them," she said, not bothering to lower her voice. "He kept plying her with drinks all night to get her shit-faced enough to take her in the bushes for a two-minute quickie neither of them will remember.

"Two minutes?"

"If that." She shrugged her shoulders, bare in some type of halter top. Her arms were covered with goosebumps. "I've had him; I should know."

"Ah." I stepped back on the path, my intrigue fading slightly.

"Now I've turned you off," she says, sadly.

"You're cold."

"Actually I prefer to think of myself as pretty hot-blooded," she grinned at me.

"I meant, I think you need a sweater."

"A pair of warm arms might do the trick."

"Are you always this direct?"

"I've waited all night for you to notice me, and finally came over when I saw you were leaving." Her eyes were enormous in her face. "I call that being patient. I'm not usually patient."

"Why did you wait?"

"I didn't want you to think I was too forward. I was trying to get *you* to notice *me.* "

"And this conversation is doing nothing to help that perception," I told her, with barely a hint of a smile to indicate my sarcasm.

Luckily, she was perceptive as well as forward.

"I'm usually very impatient," she informed me, "especially when I see something I want."

"And you decided you want me?" As much as I hoped to, I couldn't keep the skepticism out of my voice. It had been a long time since a woman approached me. In fact, other than a game of kissing tag in the fifth grade, I don't remember a female ever making the first move. Not that I was opposed; no man was. I had always been the one to begin the conversation, ask for a number, a date, for her to spend the rest of her life with me...

That last part hadn't gone well.

Six months ago, my wife of almost eight years left me.

I had married Coral when I was twenty-three and I thought we had been on track to grow old together. I was wrong.

She told me she was bored; that she needed more excitement than what I was giving her.

She wanted more romance – she wanted a happily ever after and I wasn't going to be able to give it to her.

She said she didn't think she was in love with me. That she never really loved me and had only been caught up in the romance of being married at so young an age.

I thought a lot of it had to do with our inability to conceive, mixed with our immaturity when we married. We grew up together, as we began to grow apart.

And then there was the other man. I thought that put the nail in the coffin for Coral. She had an affair and that gave her the romance and excitement she craved. I didn't bother telling her it wouldn't last. I just let her go without a fight.

I've spent the last six months regretting giving up so easily. Until now.

Until now, after I was approached by this woman, this attractive and sexy woman with this beautiful hair, wearing too much mascara, hugging herself to keep warm and...was that a tattoo on her ankle?

Having the love of your life walk away from you, claiming a lack of excitement apparently made you skeptical of the interest of other women.

"Yes," she said. There was no hint of coyness or flirtation; she held my gaze with those dark eyes. I felt like I was drowning in their depths. "I decided I wanted you the moment I saw you, saw how bored and vulnerable and alone you looked. You want to be anywhere else but here but you're a good man and told someone you'd be here, so here you are."

"You could tell that just from looking at me?" Her mention of how alone I looked caught me off guard. I thought I did quite well at hiding my feelings.

"I want to make you less lonely," she told me. "And because you look like you could use some fun," she added with a smile. "Plus, you look a little like Sean Bean and he's really hot."

I looked at her standing on the path blocking my way. That hair and her shoulders – everything down to the chipped nail polish on her toenails caught my interest. She came across as tough and slightly defiant but I sensed something more deep down.

"Do you need a ride?" I asked. I regretted asking as soon as the words were out of my mouth. I wasn't looking to get involved; I wasn't even looking for a casual hook-up. After Coral left, I decided I was fine on my own and in the six months since she left, there hadn't been anyone. I told myself that was a good thing.

My body seemed to be telling me differently now.

"I always want a ride," she said rudely, and I was so surprised I laughed.

"The least I can do is take you home," I said. "Did you come with someone?"

"Yes, but I'm not leaving with *them*."

"You're going to leave with me."

She reached out and took my hand. "That wasn't a question. You know I'm going to leave with you."

She kissed me then, standing on her tiptoes to reach my mouth. Her lips were cool and I tasted wine on her tongue as it darted into my mouth. Only our lips touched; I had the sensation if I grabbed hold of her, I would never let her go.

"Do you usually kiss strange men in the middle of the forest?" I asked her as the kiss ended.

"You're not strange men. I think you're a nice man. Do you ever kiss strange women in the forest?"

"That was a first."

"I think you should do it more often."

"To other strange women, or just you?"

"Oh, I think I'm quite enough for you," she said with a twinkle in her eye. "Let's go. I'm cold."

"What's your name?" I asked in a last-ditch effort to slow things down. I felt my night spiralling out of control.

"Does it matter? I'll tell you in the morning."

"In the morning..." I trailed off.

I let her lead me to my truck and climb in beside me. And before I could turn the key in the ignition, she was kissing me and this time I did put my arms around her and I didn't want to let go.

It had been a long time since I held a woman in my arms, but even so, I had never held a woman like Michelle. For one thing, her hands were everywhere. It seemed like she had my cock pulled out of my pants before I could count to three before I had even tried the accidental breast graze.

Apparently, things were a little different these days.

"Hey, hold on," I stammered as she leaned down over my lap. "You don't have to do that."

"Of course I don't," she said scornfully. "I *want* to. I've wanted to all night. Do you really want me to stop?"

Before I could answer before I could form a coherent thought, she had my cock in her mouth and there was no coherence at all. Six months was a long time.

She cupped my balls in her hand as she teased the tip with her tongue, licking farther and farther down the shaft. No, I didn't want her to stop, even if I could tell her to.

The only sound in the truck was my ragged breathing as she bobbed her head along my length, slowly at first, then faster and the little noises she made as she sucked me. She teased the tip with her tongue inside her mouth, and I bit back my groan.

When I felt her teeth scrape the side, I let myself place my hands on her head but didn't push down.

I kept my eyes open to keep watch for anyone leaving the party. I wouldn't want to be caught like this.

And then she moved faster and faster and I forgot about everything else. I closed my eyes and pushed down her head and let out an animal groan as I exploded inside her mouth.

"Where do you live?" I asked stiffly after I tucked myself away and she was safely strapped into the seat beside me. The blowjob had been completely unexpected and now it was awkward.

For me, at least. "I'm between places," she told me blithely.

"Where should I drop you then?"

"Your place?" she considered. "At least we don't have to worry about calling the next day."

"Are you serious?" I said before I could stop myself. Things really had changed in the years since I had married.

"I'm always serious about something like this. That was only a taste for me. Can you say you're not interested?"

I could feel her eyes on me, but I wouldn't turn to look at her. Of course I was interested and only a fool would even think about turning her down, but still, I hesitated. I didn't need any involvement. I didn't need any distractions in my life. I was doing fine on my own.

"We can see what happens after tomorrow," she said lightly, resting her hand on my leg.

I glanced down at her hand and over at her and got lost in those eyes.

Once we got back to my place, she never left.

Until she left me ten years later.

It was a challenge being with Michelle. I was hooked—physically, emotionally, everything about her, but that was the easy part. She was the most fiercely independent, infuriatingly stubborn and opinionated person I had ever met. Michelle had left home when she was sixteen and to her, taking care of herself was the number one priority. It wasn't easy convincing her I could care about her as much as she did, but I managed. She was a photographer, a talented, passionate artist and travelled a great deal. It was difficult keeping up with her, and then I stopped trying, preferring to be her home base, always waiting, keeping the home fires burning for her. She seemed to appreciate that.

Michelle had always been open and honest about her past to me, which included both men and women. Never before had I been the inexperienced one in the relationship, and hearing about her history always gave me a bit of a pause. But I accepted her past as being a part of who she was. I loved her. It was a different love from what I felt from Coral. We had been kids when we met and married and I always felt I needed to take care of her, protect her from the world.

What I felt for Michelle was all-encompassing and sometimes I wondered if I needed to be protected from her.

A few months after we had been living together, Michelle took me to a party.

She didn't tell me anything about what kind of party it was, or what to expect. In fact, I never suspected anything until I saw people pair off and disappear, at times with an entourage following, and even then I never really knew what was going on. To me, it was yet another house party, albeit one with better food and wine than what I was used to. I wasn't even sure whose house it was, but I knew they had gone all out.

"So you're with Michelle," an older man commented, handing me a bottle of beer. We had been at the party for almost an hour, and I had probably spent ten of those minutes with Michelle. She seemed very popular with this group, which I was glad to see, but it didn't make it much of a party for me.

I gave a curt nod, using the gesture to acknowledge the comment and to thank him for the beer. But then I relented, seeing as he had been the only one to start a conversation with me. I had received admiring glances and hushed comments, but that was it. There were about twenty or so people gathered, and I was in a mood where small talk was painful for me. "Joe," I volunteered.

"Joe. Nice to meet you. I'm Declan St. Clair." He offered me his hand and smiled. He was tall and broad and built like a football player.

"Did you use to play for the Roughriders?" I asked, his name and size ringing a bell.

"Ah, a fellow football lover. I don't usually get recognized at these parties. You must have played?"

"A few years at Western," I admitted. "I blew out my knee senior year and that was the end of that."

Declan patted his shoulder. "Shoulder. I tried to play through it, but it was never the same. Fun bunch of years, though."

"I bet," I grinned at him, and we discussed football for a while. Declan's aura was of a charming, well-groomed, slightly arrogant older man, but he became more approachable the more we spoke.

"So how did you meet our Michelle?" Declan asked after we had debated Toronto's chances for the Grey Cup this year.

"Your Michelle?" I raised an eyebrow at his propitiatory tone, thinking my earlier assessment of arrogance was right on.

"We've known her for a while. My wife Nathalie and I are quite fond of her."

"That's strange since she's never once mentioned you."

Declan gave a sudden, booming laugh that drew the attention of an incredibly sexy woman, who moved toward us with a smile. "She didn't say anything about us? About tonight? My love, we might have a problem here," he said to the woman.

"Hello," she said to me, catching my arm and slowly drawing her hand towards my palm, which she stroked lightly. "I'm Nathalie, your hostess for the evening. You must be Joe. Michelle told me *all* about you."

"My wife," Declan added proudly.

"So what's the problem?" I asked bluntly.

"Michelle never said anything to him about tonight," Declan told Nathalie.

"Oh, dear." But she was smiling as she spoke. "What should we do about this?"

"Do you think you might want to fill him in?" Declan asked.

Nathalie stepped back, still holding my hand, and took a long, appraising look at me. I had never felt more like a piece of meat, but I also found myself standing straighter and hoping she would like what she saw. Nathalie wasn't classically beautiful; she was an attractive woman with long, wavy hair worn loose around her face, red lipstick on a full mouth and dark, hungry eyes, but she was sexy. I would guess her age at least mid-fifties and looking at her, I found myself wondering why I had never before found older women attractive.

"I would *love* nothing more," Nathalie said, with a faint French accent. She shared a knowing glance with her husband. "You'll be fine on your own?"

"I'm sure I can find someone to amuse me." Declan clapped a hand on my shoulder with enough strength to make me wince. "Nice talking to you, Joe. I hope to see more of you."

And then Nathalie led me through the room by the hand. I had no idea what was going on. I still hadn't seen Michelle in a while, and couldn't imagine what Nathalie had to tell me. As she led me down a hallway, we were joined by another woman, a tiny brunette who looked to be a little older than me.

"Want some company?" she asked.

"Heather!" Nathalie said, kissing her on the mouth. "Of course. How perfect. Come along and meet Joe. Michelle brought him."

"Ah, Michelle," Heather said. "You know she's with Tia?"

"I *thought* they might hit it off," Nathalie said. "Let's have a look."

"What's going on?" I demanded as Nathalie pulled me into a room.

It was a bedroom, sparsely decorated save for the huge bed in the centre of the room heaped with white pillows.

"Welcome to our home," Nathalie said to me. "Occasionally we like to have parties for our friends."

"Special parties," Heather added.

"For special friends," Nathalie nodded, taking Heather by the hand and drawing her close. Then she kissed her, a deep, open-mouthed kiss.

I had never seen two women kiss like that before, not unless it was in a movie. Never live, right in front of me.

And then Nathalie drew me in, still holding Heather's hand, and kissed *me*, her tongue exploring my mouth.

"What the fuck?" I stammered as I pulled away.

"I'm surprised Michelle never told you," Heather said. She had put her hand on the small of my back as Nathalie kissed me and it began to drift lower.

"I'm not," Nathalie told me, still holding my hand. "It's never easy having that conversation, and Michelle does like easy. But I would have never said you were her type," she said, with a smile, head cocked to the side so that her hair tumbled over her shoulder.

"What's that supposed to mean?"

"Nothing bad, and I didn't mean to offend you. Michelle has always looked for playmates, nothing more. You seem so much more serious, so grown up." She cupped my chin in her hand and I can't pull away from her eyes. "She must be quite taken with you, and I can't say I blame her."

"What's going on here?" I demanded as Nathalie began to stroke my cheek. "I thought you were friends with her?"

Nathalie shrugged but didn't take away her hand. "In a way. Which is why I know this is fine with her. Joe, our parties give others a place to play. Anything goes here. Do you understand?"

"Where's Michelle?"

"I'm sure she's enjoying herself and you should be too. That's all that matters here, you see? Your enjoyment. Pleasure. Gratification. And being happy. I'd very much like to make you happy, Joe. Both Heather and I would like this. Now, do you understand?"

I was beginning to. I couldn't believe it, but I was beginning to understand what was going on. "Is this some kind of orgy?" I asked bluntly.

Nathalie grimaced. "I've never liked that word. Declan and I have an open relationship, and so do many of our friends."

"Where's Michelle?" My voice sounded gruff.

"She's right here. If you'd like to take a look." Nathalie smiled at Heather and then took us both by the hand to the mirror on the wall.

It wasn't a mirror. It was a window looking into the next room. I found myself looking at Michelle – Michelle on the bed with another woman.

"Oh...shit," I breathed.

Michelle was naked and lying spread-eagled on the bed. The other woman was still dressed in a blouse and underwear and crouched between Michelle's legs.

"That's Tia," Nathalie said conversationally like it wasn't uncommon to watch women pleasure each other. "She's lovely."

In fact, I was beginning to think it wasn't uncommon to see something like that here at all. It was incredibly hot and sexy as I watched, I could feel myself grow hard. I wasn't surprised to see this side of Michelle; there had been so much I sensed she had wanted to tell me but held back. And even knowing some of what she had experienced in the past, I had accepted it – her – and never really thought of what she had done, or where, to get that experience.

Michelle had brought me to this party, knowing she would be able to be with another woman, knowing I would be able to do the same.

What did that mean for our relationship? What did that mean for us?

"We're all here for the excitement," Heather told me. "No one judges and nothing goes any further than this house."

Coral had never thought I was exciting enough for her. If Michelle had brought me here, it was obvious she didn't feel the same way. It wasn't that *she* was looking for more; we both could find it here.

"Michelle has decided to spend some time with Tia tonight," Nathalie explained. "She'll still go home with you. In the meantime, *we* were hoping to spend some time with *you*." Both Nathalie and Heather smiled invitingly at me.

At me.

Both of them.

"Or you could leave," Nathalie suggested gently. "If this isn't something you'd be comfortable with. There's no pressure. No strings. Just...enjoy us."

I looked from Nathalie to Heather – two very attractive women who wanted me. Then I looked through the window again to see Michelle, her expression full of lust as Tia pleasured her with her mouth.

I'd never seen anything like it.

"What's it going to be?" Nathalie said briskly.

I glanced back at her, at my hand that she was still holding. Then I looked at her mouth.

I wasn't going anywhere. My brain might not have fully realized everything, but my body knew enough to stay.

With a delighted smile, Nathalie pulled me away from the window and over to the bed. I got one last glance though, enough to see Michelle's face contorted, clearly in the throes of an orgasm.

"Why don't you take his pants off?" Nathalie suggested to Heather, as she placed a hand at the back of my head, stroking my neck as she took one of my hands that were hanging limply at my side, and put it on her breast.

Instinctively, I squeezed. It was full and firm, and her nipple hardened under my hand. And then she kissed me again.

I wasn't conscious of Heather as Nathalie kissed me, both of my hands full of her breasts until I realized my pants were off and heard her voice.

"My turn," she said with a giggle.

I tore myself away from Nathalie to see Heather standing before me, naked. Her body was tight and compact, with small firm breasts and enormous nipples. Before I could get a good look at them, she yanked my shirt off and then pulled my head down to those nipples. One was in my mouth before I realized what was happening.

I licked and sucked and teased her nipples with my teeth, Heather's hands holding my head firm. One of my hands cupped a breast, the other wandered over her body – her slim waist, the faint curve of her hips, her firm backside.

And then I felt hands on my back, my waist, and the feel of a body pressed against me. Hands stroked my cock.

"Get him on the bed," I heard Nathalie's voice as if from a distance.

I was ushered to the bed, and laid down against the pillows. My mind was frazzled, befuddled, but my cock was rock hard. Heather and Nathalie both dropped a kiss on my mouth – I tried to catch Nathalie, but she evaded me with a smile— and then beginning at my shoulders, the two of them began kissing their way down my chest.

I realized I was holding my breath and let it out with a huff. This was every man's dream and it was happening to me, now, while my girlfriend was in the next room with another woman.

That realization soured my enjoyment, but only a little.

Nathalie and Heather reached my stomach and as she was dropping kisses around my belly button, Nathalie grasped my cock firmly with her hand.

"I was hoping to end up here with you," she told me, before bending over me and licking from the base of my shaft to the tip.

And then there were two tongues.

Two mouths on my cock, one after the other, taking me in their warm mouths.

Eventually, I couldn't tell them apart. I laid back against the pillows and closed my eyes.

One used her tongue as she slid her mouth down the length of me, twirling my tip. The other sucked as hard as she could so it felt like I was being drawn in, before she took the entire length of me in her mouth. I touched the back of her throat.

One used teeth.

One licked my tip like it was her favourite lollipop.

Wet mouths, warm breaths, low murmurs I couldn't understand.

And then they stopped.

"Our turn," Heather said brightly.

They pulled me down the bed so I was lying flat on my back. And then Heather crawled up the bed, gave me another kiss and crouched over me, lowering her pussy onto my waiting tongue. I steadied her, catching the backs of her legs and thrust my tongue into her wetness.

"You look so sexy like that," Nathalie told her. "I can't wait to fuck you."

I wasn't sure who she was referring to. I concentrated on tonguing Heather; running my tongue through her cleft, tasting her wetness and hearing her gasps and moans and feeling her shivers as I reached her clit.

I was sucking her clit between flickers of my tongue when my cock was caught inside something wonderfully warm and wet.

"I really like your cock," Nathalie said in a husky voice as she lowered herself onto me.

For a moment, I lost my concentration as Nathalie began to move. Up and down, riding the length of me, her hands braced on my chest.

"Ride him, cowboy," Heather said, her laugh checked by her cry as I regained my concentration and thrust into her with my tongue. "Oh, Nat, he's good."

"He has to come back. Michelle's a lucky girl."

And that's the last thing I hear them say. Nathalie began to move harder and faster, lifting herself so that only my tip was inside her, before slamming back down. It felt so good, I was having difficulty focusing on Heather, but her cries and moans would bring my attention back to her pussy. I found the rhythm she seemed to enjoy – lots of tonguing her

clit, circle and suck, with some forays inside her. I thought she might
be getting close to coming from the sound and frequency of her cries. I
could hear Nathalie's deeper moans as she rode me and prayed she was
close as well because I didn't think I could hold out much longer.

I maneuvered my hand between Heather's legs and thrust two fingers
inside her pussy as I sucked her clit, sending her over the edge. I could
hear her cries as she came, muffled by her shaking legs as she rocked above
me.

When she was finally still, she climbed off me and I was faced with the
sight of Nathalie riding me with a fierce determination. I grasped her
hips and thrust upward with everything I had.

"Oh, god," she cried out loudly.

Heather put her hand on Nathalie's pussy and began rubbing her clit
as I continued to drive upward into her.

"That's it," she moaned. "Fuck me just like that...Heather, please!
Don't stop!"

I felt her pussy contract around me, which put me over the edge and
I thrust one final time.

"Oh, my god," Heather cried with delight. "That was *so* good."

I opened my eyes to see Nathalie smiling with satisfaction down at me.
"Think you might come back another time?" she asked.

I wasn't sure what to tell her.

How did you like learning more about my naughty neighbours??

Don't think I've left out Melissa and Paige! They get their own story
as well!

Melissa

AN INTERLUDE

ANNA ELLIS

THREE BIRDS PRESS

Melissa: An Interlude

I've always thought it was the husband's duty to provide the necessary tools to fully celebrate Valentine's Day and so far in the eight years we've been married, Mahak has fulfilled this duty to my complete satisfaction.

But this year, he really stepped up.

Last week he told me that he had to attend a birthday party for his boss on the 14th and would like me to go with him. To his credit, he apologized, knowing that my plans had not included doing some serious butt kissing of his manager, although I am very good at it. He knew I wanted a nice evening out, at a downtown restaurant, possibly staying over a hotel with a Jacuzzi, where we would indulge in some serious sexapades.

I don't think I ask for much. Mahak and I have been married for eight years now – nine in June – and every year Mahak makes an effort on Valentine's Day. I guess I've come to expect it. Mahak's a pretty romantic guy anyway, what with the flowers on special occasions, spoiling me on my birthday and the whole arrangement with the neighbours.

I know – most wouldn't call allowing your wife to have sex with other men *romantic* but it's the way he does it. He knows I have a high sex drive and that he satisfies me completely. But Mahak also knows that coming to him as a virgin when I was twenty-one meant I missed out on *a lot*. Jacey says having lots of experience isn't as good as it seems, but then she's lost count of all the men she's been with. She's the only one I know who is more adventurous than me.

I never got the wild teenage years, making out in the back seats of cars and under the bleachers. I didn't get to experiment in my 20s with everything and anything because I was already with Mahak and he was amazing. We did lots of experimenting on our own. But when given the opportunity to do a little swinging with the neighbours, Mahak was all for it because he knew that's what I needed.

I call that romantic because Mahak was thinking of what *I* wanted, not himself. Why would he want to have sex with Wendy, Paige, and Molly before they moved? I'm the best he's ever going to get. I might have started out slow, but I've more than made up for it in a big way.

And I had been planning on showing Mahak on Valentine's Day. After years of refusing to give blowjobs, I've been practicing my technique on Joe and I'm ready to blow my husband's mind with the best blow job ever. It just took a little mind over matter to stop letting the taste bother me, but I think I'm okay with it now. And tonight, I was going to demonstrate on Mahak. It was going to be my Valentine's Day present to him and I know it would have been exactly what he wants

But no. No blowjob for him now. We have to go to Burlington for a 60th birthday party. Who has a birthday party on Valentine's Day anyway?

Mahak must have known he was in my bad books because when I woke up on the 14th, it was with the sensation of Mahak's fingers between my legs.

Mahak leaves for work just after 7 in the morning, but I'm always up much earlier than that so I can work out. It's not easy keeping this body in tip-top shape and every year and every kid makes it a little more difficult. So to have Mahak wake me rather than the alarm was a welcome change. We hadn't made love the night before – even though I had wanted to – because I was irritated about having to go to the party. Sex is an almost daily occurrence with Mahak and me, and when it doesn't happen, I miss it.

I sleep naked so there's nothing to impede the progress of Mahak's clever fingers between my legs. I'm on my stomach when I feel the touch of his hand stroking my ass before burrowing between my thighs. I'm not quite awake when I instinctively lift and widen my legs to give him better access. His long, strong fingers head straight for my clit.

"Mmm," I moan, turning my head to smiling sleepily at my husband. I'm always struck by how handsome he is. I love how his dark eyes look at me when he wants me. Which is most of the time, it seems.

Mahak smiles at me, showing lots of white teeth. "Good morning, beautiful."

"If this is your way of making it up to me for not taking me out tonight, you'd better not stop," I order. I enjoy the sensation of his fingers in my pussy but decide I want more and roll over on my back and look at him expectantly.

"Your wish is my command," Mahak says. There's a sudden chill as Mahak whips the blankets off my nakedness but I'm warmed as he leans over to kiss me quickly. Ignoring my breasts, he heads for my pussy, bringing my knees up and replacing his fingers with something even better. He begins to lick me with long languorous strokes of his tongue.

"You are the very best," I sigh.

And he is, even with my limited experience. Well, I've had Jackson, Colin and Joe, that is. And now Dominic. And Jason and Molly. I'm doing my best to make up for what I've missed in my younger years and I'm lucky we have the kind of neighbours we do. Especially Tia. Tia is very talented, and so is Joe – almost as good as Mahak, but Mahak...everyone agrees I'm one lucky girl.

His tongue is thick and Gene Simmons-long and he can really work it. Slowly at first, Mahak licks from my ass to my clit again and again, before thrusting inside. And then he begins to suck my clit, pausing often to circle it slowly with his tongue.

I love oral sex. I like it with both men and women, but Mahak *is* the best.

His tongue is sure and strong and he knows what I want. I like it when he thrusts it inside, as hard as a small penis. I love it when he sucks my clit in his mouth like he's doing *right now*!

"That's so *good*," I breathe, with both hands on the back of his dark head.

I can tell he's smiling as he licks my pussy. He likes it as much as I do.

As his tongue moves against my clit, quickly now, I'm almost at the edge, pushing myself against his eager mouth and he knows it. He knows when I'm about to come.

I feel it beginning in my core, spreading relentlessly through my body, like sinking into the best bath ever.

Suddenly, I arch my back and cry out, careful not to wake the kids.

Mahak stops as I come and forcefully turns me over. As soon as I'm on fours, he's inside me with a violent thrust. Mahak isn't the most gentle of lovers, but that's all right. If I want gentle, there's always Joe or Tia...or Wendy. The last time at Tia's, I had been with Wendy and Joe and it seemed like my girl-on-girl lessons had certainly paid off.

I'm not sure if it's because I'm thinking of Wendy or just Mahak's incredible prowess as a cocksman, but I start to come again right away.

The feel of his thick cock inside me is one of my favourite things, almost as good as his eating my pussy. Knowing he always wants me, anytime, is the most amazing thing about our marriage.

His hands grip my hips and he pumps against me. Mahak has the most amazing control, but this morning he's quick and fast and hard, thrusting in and out. I can tell from his breathing he's close to coming and reach between my legs with my hand to help myself along. Fingering my clit, I come again. It's more intense this time, and Mahak thrusts powerfully enough that I pitch forward and we come together.

I love making love with my husband.

Despite the fun during my morning wake-up, I'm still not in the best mood when we get to the party later that night, although I do make sure I look my best. Little tight red dress, hair blown out, makeup perfectly applied. I don't want to be at this party, but I go without making too much of a fuss because I will do just about anything for Mahak.

The birthday party is for Mahak's senior manager, William Burgess and is held at his house, right on the shores of Lake Ontario. As we pull into the circular drive, Mahak lets out a low whistle under his breath.

"Nice place."

"It's all right," I say dismissively, even though it's anything but. It's a huge house, almost palatial with Roman columns standing on guard before the door. Apparently, senior managers do well for themselves. We don't have houses like this in our neighbourhood.

But then, they won't have neighbours like ours.

As the valet helps me from the car, he smiles at the shortness of my skirt. I ignore him. Flirting with the valet drivers isn't on my list of how to make this night get any better, even though he is cute.

The door is held open for us by a black-clad servant. "Welcome. Let me take your coats," he says, helping me shrug out of my plain black pea coat. His eyes pop when he gets a full-eye view of my dress. It does make my breasts look spectacular.

"Mr. Burgess is in the study," he informs us, adding, "Can we get you a glass of champagne?" as another servant steps up with a tray of glasses.

"Of course," I tell them, helping myself to two and handing one to Mahak with a grudging smile. From first impressions of the house, maybe this party isn't going to be too dreadful after all. I can smell delicious food in the distance along with expensive cologne and the noise of party guests is a loud hum, broken by a sudden peal of laughter.

Mahak puts his hand on the small of my back and ushers me to the sweeping staircase, away from the laughter and good smells.

"The party is that way," I tell him, balking at the stairs. "Where are we going?"

"Will is in the study. We'll go say hello first."

"Have you been here before?" I ask as we climb the stairs. I can see the party below us, guests clustered in groups, holding glasses and enjoying themselves.

"A few times," he admitted. "I remember where the study is."

"It's a beautiful house," I concede.

"I know it's not the Valentine's Day you hoped for but I think you'll have a good time tonight." Mahak smiles at me, his dark eyes crinkling at the corners. My husband is a handsome devil and I decide to tell him so.

"Thank you, princess," he says, his eyes dark and soulful with a hint of promise. "You look especially lovely tonight." His eyes linger on my cleavage. "I'm sure I can find a way to make it up to you."

"Oh, I think you can find several ways," I tell him archly as we reach a closed door at the top of the staircase. I clink my glass against his and reach up on my tiptoes to give him a kiss. This leads to another, and another and soon Mahak has me pressed tightly against him, his hand moulding my dress against my ass.

"We should probably go in," Mahak says, drawing away from me reluctantly. His kisses have taken my breath away from me. I'm glad it's still that way, even after eight years of marriage. He still excites me.

"Do we have to? Empty hallway, lots of rooms..."

"You'll have fun tonight," he assures me, with one last kiss.

"Promise? What if I don't?"

"Trust me." Then he opens the door for me.

I'm not exactly sure what makes a room a study, but I can bet there's no studying going on in here. It's a massive space with a roaring fire at the end of the room, couches set in front of it, countless shelves built into the walls, and an elevated billiard table in the centre of the room. For such a large space, however, there are surprisingly few people. A small group stands in front of the fire. I stop by the table, running my hand along the edge.

"Are we here to play pool or to party?" I wonder aloud, playing with the eight ball alone on the table.

A handsome, older man detaches himself from the group and comes over to us with a welcoming smile. "Most of the guests are in the living room," he explains. "I much prefer a small, more intimate gathering, but there are so many who need to be appeased by an invitation. Bryce at the door knows who to bring to me here."

"I feel special that we made the cut," I say coyly.

"There's no doubt in my mind you would have made the cut," the man says admiringly. Taking my hand, he plucks the ball I'm holding and holds my hand tight in both of his. His hands are warm with long fingers. "You must be Melissa. I've heard much about you. I'm Will."

"Princess, this is William Burgess," Mahak says.

"It's nice to meet you," I say hesitantly, glancing around the room again. I think I'd rather go back downstairs. Five people stand huddled in front of the fire, and all are staring at us. "Happy birthday," I add. Mahak hasn't told me anything about Will, other than he's a good boss.

Finding out Mahak has been in his house, and we've made some special guest list makes me uncertain. I don't like feeling that way. I take a sip of my champagne for courage.

"It's lovely to meet you." Still holding my hand, Will's eyes drift over my face, travelling down my body like he's assessing it. Instinctively I pull in my already flat stomach and push out my chest. He stares at me for longer than what is polite, his eyes lingering on my cleavage, my legs, my mouth. I don't mind being checked out, but it's rude to be so obvious about it. So I decide to check him out, forgetting about being subtle, which is never my strong point anyway.

Will Burgess is the stereotype for a 'good-looking older man'; tall, tanned with short salt-and-pepper hair and piercing blue eyes. His eyes would be his best feature if they didn't look so hard. He looks unyielding, which is probably what makes him so successful. He's really sexy for an older man, with a beautiful, kissable mouth.

Why would I think he has a kissable mouth? The man must be in his early sixties and I've never been attracted to older men. Plus, I'm sure he has a wife...

That's not always a problem.

"You smell wonderful," I blurt out. His heady cologne surrounds us.

"She's as lovely as you said she was," Will finally tells Mahak, tearing his eyes away from me. I can tell he likes what he sees and once again I'm glad I made such an effort.

"What else did you say about me? Don't believe everything you hear," I tell Will with a coy smile.

Will's face falls, but he keeps a hold of my hand. "Oh no? That would be a shame."

"What did you say?" I demand Mahak but Will doesn't give him a chance to answer.

"Let's introduce you around, shall we? As much as I'd love to keep you in a corner talking to me all evening, I'm sure the others would be upset. Come." And without a word of protest, Will leads me past the pool table to the group standing before the fire.

Right away I notice the woman standing close to the fire. She's tall with light blonde hair I suspect can't be natural, and an unlined face that is quite lovely. But it's her eyes that draw me in; huge eyes, so dark they seem to be black; observing everything but letting nothing out.

She reminds me of Tia. The best way I can describe Tia is that I could picture her as a queen. I can see her with a crown, standing in front of her people, who would all adore her. She's got that regal sort of appeal to her. Of course, she loses that imposing imperialness when she's having sex with you, although she's still quite commanding.

The blonde woman reminds me of Tia, and sparks my interest, but Will leads me to the other woman in the group instead.

"Melissa, this is Serena."

There is no regal bearing to this one. Serena looks like the royal concubine, hot and ready to go. With a body that's *almost* as good as mine, she's flaunting it in a little black lace dress that is shorter and tighter than my red one. With the amount of caramel-coloured skin I can see through the fabric, I doubt she has anything underneath.

Serena doesn't say anything to me, only nods her head sullenly. She seems to be playing with something in her mouth.

"Serena," Will says quietly but it sounds like a warning. He holds my hand tightly.

"Hi," she says quickly to me and smiles. It's not sincere.

I slowly look her up and down. "Hello," I say dismissively with a curl of my lip and turn away from her. Two can play this game, and nobody puts Melissa in a corner.

"*You're* going to be fun," one of the men steps forward, shielding me from Serena's bitch-like stare. He kisses me full on the lips. "I'm Dawson. Let's start this."

He's very pretty and friendly and I think he might be gay. "This is the terrible twosome, Pierce and Hugh," Dawson tells me, referring to the two men beside Serena and curling his arm around the shorter man's shoulder. "This is Pierce." Will finally releases my hand, leaving me with Dawson and I feel the chill. I want him to stay with me but he moves to Mahak's side. They begin to talk in voices too low for me to hear.

"What's so terrible about you?" I ask the two distractedly, trying to hear what Will is saying to Mahak.

"You'll just *have* to find out," Dawson winks at me. I smile hesitantly. I hate to admit it, but Serena's welcome – or lack of it – threw me off my stride. Women often have a problem with me but usually, I can deal with it. Men are always easier to handle. Give them a good look at my breasts, a few smiles and they're putty in my hands. These three seem like no exception.

"It's nice to meet you. Do you work together?" I glance at Dawson for confirmation, but it's Hugh who answers.

"Not us. We're neighbours. I live up the street."

I stare at Hugh. "You're joking."

"No. Why, do you have something against neighbours? Will throws the best parties. I hope you'll enjoy yourself as much as we will," Hugh said. He is middle height, but with a barrel-like chest and a friendly, non-threatening smile, sort of like Colin.

It has to be a coincidence. Doesn't it?

"Can't see why I wouldn't. I always like to have fun."

"Then you're the perfect guest for us. Let's get you a drink." Hugh easily separates me from Dawson and leads me by the hand to a table across the room. I glance back to see Mahak still whispering with Will, and Dawson, Pierce and Serena staring after me.

"So tell me about yourself, little Melissa," Hugh says. He pulls a dripping bottle from an ice bucket. "More Champagne?"

"Please." I finish the drink I have with a giant gulp, probably not the best way to drink champagne. Hugh refills the glass and I watch the bubbles dissipate in the glass as he hands it to me. I take a sip right away.

"Does anyone call you Missy?" Hugh wonders.

"Not if they expect me to answer," I retort sharply.

"You're a spicy one, aren't you?" he muses.

"I like to think so."

"I like that."

"So do I? Who's the blonde?" I ask bluntly.

"That's Tandy. She's Will's second – no, is it third? – wife," Hugh tells me.

"Third wife?" I look back at the blonde woman standing by herself in front of the fire, ignoring everything around her and staring at one of the bookshelves, a glass of clear liquid in her hand.

"She doesn't say much," Hugh explains, following my gaze. "But she's...nice."

"Really? Looks to me there should be a fourth wife."

Hugh gives a quick laugh and quickly smothers it. "No, Will's happy with her. She's very...tolerant."

"What is there to be tolerant about? Married to a sexy, successful man, and in this house? What does she have to look so miserable about?"

"She's not miserable, she's...aloof. I'm sure she's very happy at this moment."

"She really looks it," I say sarcastically. The only reason I have to be dissecting Tandy like this is that I don't like being ignored, especially by people I find intriguing. Even with only a glance at Tandy, she sparked my interest and she ignored me.

"You'll see what she's like soon enough," Hugh promises me. And then," You think Will is sexy?"

"Sure. He has amazing eyes. And he smells good."

"I smell good," Hugh says, moving closer.

"You smell good, too," I say to appease him.

"I have nice eyes. And a nice house," he continues.

"Are you jealous of Will?" I wonder.

Hugh laughs easily. "Of course not. I love the guy. He's like a brother to me. But he gets all the attention at nights like this."

"But it's his birthday," I say carefully. "And it's his house."

"Yes, it is," Hugh agrees heavily. "And it's an impressive house. And Will is an impressive guy."

"He is. But I know what you mean," I tell him conspiratorially, thinking of how I feel when Jacey is in the same room as I am. I want to be around her; I want her to like me, but I want everyone else to like me more than they like her.

Childish, I'm sure, but that's how it is.

"Anyway," Hugh says, returning to our discussion. "Tandy is good for Will. Very accepting and adventurous."

"I'm adventurous," I tell him quickly.

"I'm sure you are, or you wouldn't be here."

I frown. "It's a birthday party, not an adventure."

Hugh looks at me quizzically. "What did your husband tell you about Will?"

"Not much, actually. Is there something I should know?"

Hugh shakes his head quickly. "There's lots to know, but I'm not the one to tell you." And with that cryptic remark, he leads me back to the group.

The evening passes quickly and in a bit of a blur. Will and his friends do everything they can to make me feel welcome, although I do notice quite a few sideways glances and knowing looks making their way around the room. The men are quite admiring of me, and each of them makes a point to tell me how wonderful I look. I have to admit I love the attention.

They also keep my glass topped up. I'm not normally much of a drinker and do my best to moderate my intake but the champagne is quite delicious. In fact, the entire evening is going much better than expected. I don't think I'll have a need to punish Mahak for insisting we come tonight, although it might be fun to try. I might save that for another night, seeing as Mahak doesn't seem to be in any hurry to leave. In fact, he seems quite comfortable here.

We've moved to the conversation pit by the pool table. I'm pressed into a corner of the couch with Serena close beside me and Dawson perched on the arm on my other side. Dawson is beautiful, with silky blonde hair that looks in need of a cut and brilliant green eyes. He keeps touching me like we're old friends and it's true I feel comfortable with him, but I'm not sure if he's gay or straight.

It doesn't matter to me, but it might to Serena. She looks like she's ready to eat him alive. She reminds me a little of Jacey but has none of my friend's aloofness or hesitation.

Is Jacey my friend? I've fucked her, my husband has fucked her and we'd both like to do so again, but I've never considered whether she is my friend or not. Wendy and Paige are my friends, and of course Tia is. I share more with Tia than anyone. But Jacey...

I liked making her come. I liked how she tasted and how she begged me for it.

I wonder if she'd want to have another threesome. Or maybe just me.

"What are you thinking about?" Serena surprises me by asking.

"What do you mean?"

"You like you're thinking dirty thoughts."

"How can you tell?" I gasp. Serena laughs. "Not that I was."

"Too bad. I like dirty thoughts."

"You're a dirty girl," Dawson tells her appreciatively.

"That's why you love me the best." They lean over me and kiss. It's not just a peck on the cheek either but a lingering, open-mouth kiss and I think I see a hint of tongue. I can't look away.

"Do you like to watch?" Serena asks me as she pulls back.

"When you do that in front of me it's hard not to," I retort.

Serena laughs. "Want me to kiss you, too?"

I glance at her mouth, watching it curve up in a suggestive smile, taunting me. Normally I would take the dare, but tonight I'm not so sure.

"Come on," Serena urges. "You know you want it." Her tongue flits out and I see a glimpse of silver. "Tongue ring," she says, sticking it further out for my inspection. "All the girls love it."

"Girls?" I ask despite myself.

"And boys. Both," she says. She puts her hand on my thigh, right at the hem of my dress, her fingers dangling over the gap between my legs. I fight not to open them. "What's your thing?"

"I don't have a *thing*," I say with difficulty.

"Oh, you do. I don't think you're one of those who haven't realized it yet. You know what you want, and I bet you go and get it." Serena holds my eyes, her tongue flickering in and out of her mouth. "So do I."

I have an urge to tell her just what I want, and what I've had, but resist. One of the vows we made when Mahak and I began this arrangement with the neighbours was to not discuss it with anyone. I turn away from Serena with difficulty and she laughs knowingly.

"I like to watch," Dawson offers.

"I know you do, baby," Serena smiles affectionately at him. "Me, I like participating."

"I know you do, baby," Dawson mocks her.

Serena's hand is warm on my leg. She begins to stroke my bare thigh with her fingers. I watch them curiously, like it isn't my leg, like it doesn't feel as if there is a string connecting Serena's hand to my groin, so that whenever she moves her finger, I get a jolt of excitement straight to my pussy.

"I really like this dress," Dawson tells me, leaning over me so that he's looking right down my cleavage. Now his hand is on my shoulder, his fingers tracing the edge of my dress from my shoulder to the swell of my breast.

Both of them are touching me and I'm having difficulty breathing. What's going on here? A few suggestive comments, an innocent touch and I'm suddenly as excited as a sixteen-year-old faced with a topless cheerleader. *I'm* the one who comes up with all the fun and games, and now it's like *I'm* being initiated into some sexual society. But that can't be what's going on here.

Can it?

Is this just an evening of play, like Tia's, only more high-end? Are we gathered here for the purpose of having sex with each other? Or am I just paranoid because that's what we do in our neighbourhood on Saturday nights?

Who would I want to have sex with?

I glance over at Mahak, who is deep in conversation with Will and Pierce. The men are so attractive with an aura of charisma around them. I suspect they're quite wealthy as well.

I'm proud of Mahak for being included.

Hugh is sitting across from us on the couch beside the silent Tandy. She's breath-taking, with her long blonde hair and porcelain white skin in sharp contrast to those eyes. I keep glancing at her to see if her lips have moved if her expression has changed at all, but nothing does. Only her eyes, which keep flicking from face to face.

I catch her looking at me quite a bit.

The men have finally finished their conversation and I half expect, half-want Mahak to suggest we call it a night, but instead, Will stands and holds out a hand to me. Dawson plucks my glass from my hand and Serena gives me a shove. Confused, I rise and stand beside him.

"Thank you all for coming to my party. I wanted to make sure you had a chance to get to know Melissa, this evening, Mahak's lovely wife. Isn't she exquisite?" he says admiringly, curling his arm around my waist, his fingers grazing the underside of my breast.

"Lovely," Hugh smiles at me.

"Beautiful," Dawson declares. He's finishing my champagne with a mischievous grin.

"She looks delicious," Serena says, staring at me with a predatory smile. I feel a tiny curl of apprehension in my stomach.

Or is it excitement?

I glance at Mahak, who is looking at me proudly.

I'm still not sure what's going on, but I'm not about to stop it.

"Now, would you mind coming over here with me?" Will asks, leading me to the billiard table and helping me step up the platform.

"Are we playing pool?" I ask stupidly.

"No. Not pool." He puts his hand on my shoulder, the same place Dawson had and caresses it, trailing the back of his hand down my arm, sending goosebumps through me. He finishes the little gesture by kissing my hand. "I take it Mahak didn't tell you of our little arrangement."

"No." I try and sound annoyed rather than confused.

"And that was the first test. Well done, my friend," Will smiles over my head at Mahak, who, along with the rest of the group, has followed us to the table.

"What's going on?" I finally demand.

Will runs his finger along the top of my dress, slowly dipping under the fabric, skimming the tops of my breasts. "Nothing. Unless you want it. And I have a feeling, sweet Melissa, you will want it."

"I'd like to unzip your dress?" Will asks in a low voice. "It's a lovely dress. Fits you perfectly. Do you mind?"

Before I answer, I look over my shoulder at Mahak with a question in my eyes. He gives me a smile and a shrug of his shoulders but it's his eyes that convince me. They're dark and smouldering, the same as when he's about to give me unimaginable pleasure with his tongue.

Whatever these people are into, Mahak is prepared to go along with it.

That's all I need.

I nod.

Will takes his time with my dress, running his hands down my back, moulding the fabric against my bum, and skimming his fingers past the short hem onto the bare backs of my legs. By the time Will begins to pull the zipper down, my breath has already quickened. Mahak loves how easily I get excited.

I look at each of the faces in turn as Will helps me off with my dress, seeing admiration in their eyes, approval and desire. Lust. By the time I'm standing on the platform, wearing only my lace thong, I doubt I've ever felt as wanted as I do right then.

I'm standing in front of seven people, who, I'm betting, would love to fuck me.

The only thing I can't figure out is who is going to.

Still standing facing the group, I feel Will cup my breasts from behind, toying with my nipples.

"Beautiful," Will whispers, burying his face in the spot where my neck meets my shoulder. He keeps one hand on my breasts, fondling and kneading each in turn and the other wraps around my waist and pulls me back against him. I can feel his hardness against the small of my back and he pushes himself against me.

"More," calls out a strangled voice from the group, either Hugh or Pierce.

Will slides his hand down my flat stomach. As he slips his hand between my legs, I open them slightly when he presses his palm against my panties.

Is it going to be Will? Right here in front of everyone?

I'm not sure how I feel about that. I've never done that before, had someone fuck me while others watched. I've had threesomes, of course, but that's different. *This* feels different. This feels...

Exciting. I'm excited, as Will can tell. His fingers are slowly exploring between my legs, still with his hands on my breast. I can feel his breath on my neck.

"I think that's enough for you," Serena calls. Will laughs and kisses my neck.

"Do you blame me? She's perfect, so soft and supple and these breasts..." Both hands return to cup my breasts and Will tugs on one of my nipples. He presses against me once more then steps back. "But I have my orders. Would you like first turn, my dear Serena?"

"I would. Help her onto the table please, Will."

Before I could think of anything to say – *Serena? First turn?* – Will has lifted me onto the pool table and Serena joins us on the platform. I sit primly on the edge of the table, for once unsure of myself. I'm always in control but here, now...I have no idea what to expect. For someone usually so adventurous and ready to experiment, I'm feeling more than a little apprehensive.

I think it might be adding to my excitement.

"Have you been with a woman before?" Serena asks me in her husky voice. She stands in front of me, forcing me to spread my legs so she can stand between them.

"Of course." I try for bravado to mask my unease.

"Too bad," she gives me the predatory smile again. "I love being the first." She runs her hands along my thighs and Will melts away, joining the others watching.

I think I might enjoy being watched.

"You have an amazing body," Serena says conversationally as she runs her fingers along my outer thighs.

"Thank you."

"You must work out. These have been helped, haven't they?" She nods at my breasts, her fingers constantly.

"Two kids," I retort.

"Don't get defensive, I think they look amazing but not for me. I go for this," Serena says, walking her fingers to the apex of my legs. "I like pussy. I like it a lot."

There's nothing I can think of to say to that.

"Do you want me to kiss you?"

I'm not sure where she is referring to kissing, but I nod. There's no turning back now, even if I wanted to. And I don't.

Serena leans forward and gently touches my lips with hers. For someone so aggressive, the kiss is gentle and sweet. I lean into her, enjoying
the feel of her mouth on mine, my hands gripping the edge of the table,
not wanting to give Serena the satisfaction of touching her. I'm feeling
increasingly out of control here and I need to have some semblance of
power over the situation, even if it's something as small as not putting
my arms around her, and pulling her close to me.

Serena moans against my mouth, and draws back. "Nice," she
breathes. "You might know what you're doing."

"I do," I retort.

"We'll see about that. You're with me now. Put your leg up," she
orders.

Glancing over at the group – who are all avidly watching us on the
pool table – I pull one leg up the edge of the table. I'm still wearing
my thong, but there's not much fabric covering so my pussy is open and
available to Serena. And everyone else watching.

"She's fearless," Hugh says approvingly.

"Great choice," Dawson tells Will, who pats Mahak on the back.
There's not a flicker of regret on Mahak's face. If there was – would I
have stopped things? If I thought he didn't want me to do this?

He brought me here so obviously Mahak knew what was going to
happen. He knew I'd be okay with it. He knows I like to play.

I lean back on my arms, nervous and excited and...very excited. I
haven't felt like this since the first time with Tia, or the first Saturday
night where no one knew what to expect, but we all wanted it.

I want this. Whatever this is going to be.

With her middle finger, Serena smoothes the lace of my thong between my lips, over and over so soon it's wet through. I wait for her to
take them off – I *want* her to take them off – but she doesn't. Instead,
she bends her head and begins licking me through the delicate fabric.

There's an added friction as the material rubs against me. She thrusts her tongue inside me, its progress checked by my thong.

"Take them off," I whisper.

"You're demanding," Serena says. "I don't like to be told what to do."

"Please," I beg.

"No."

Instead, she pushes the tiny scrap of lace aside and pushes a finger inside me. "Does she like to make noise?" she asks Mahak over her shoulder.

"Yes," he replies.

"Not with me," Serena says. "If you make a sound, I'll stop," she tells me, moving her finger inside me. "Do you understand?"

"Mm –" As she removes her finger, I stop and nod instead.

"Good girl," she nods her approval and bends her head, pulling my ass towards her so I'm perched on the very edge of the table. I lean back farther on my arms and tilt my pelvis to her waiting mouth.

My first thought as Serena begins to tongue me, is that this isn't her first time doing this. This woman knows exactly what she's doing and seems to know exactly what I want. Plus, the tongue ring feels really good.

Slowly, ever so slowly she licks between my lips with a feather-light touch. Her tongue probes inside me, as hard as a small penis. I press my pussy forward, desperate for more.

She doesn't give me more. She's teasing me, with the barest flickers of her tongue, spreading my lips with her fingers so she can have better access, but not doing much of anything. I want to tell her what to do and how to do it, but I remember her orders and I don't want her to stop. I want more, and the inability to command is so frustrating!

She's so close to my clit, I can feel her breath on it. Finally, she wiggles her tongue against it lightly, carelessly, like she has no regard for what I want. I bite down on my lip to stifle a moan as she flicks the tip and licks it. I can feel the hardness of her piercing.

Suddenly she sucks hard on my clit with her mouth. This time I can't stop from moaning loudly.

"That's it," Serena says, lifting her head. "You can't be quiet."

"I can," I gasp, frustrated from wanting her touch. "I will."

"Nope," she says, hopping off the platform. "Next."

I watch open-mouthed, open-legged as Pierce and Hugh both move forward. "You first," Hugh invites. "If you don't mind, I'll watch for a bit."

"I wouldn't be here if I did," Pierce says with a grin to Hugh, before smiling down at me. "Poor baby. Serena left you hanging, didn't she? Let's see if I can help you with that. Let's get these off you first, though." He slides off my thong before lifting my other leg onto the table as Hugh helps me lay back on the table.

"These breasts are amazing," Hugh says, running his hands across them.

Pierce has already dived between my legs and doesn't reply.

Does everyone get to try me?

When Mahak suggested we come to the party, he didn't say one word about it being like this. Would I have still come if he had?

Probably. Sexually, I'm up for anything, although being sampled by everyone was never on my fantasy list.

Maybe it should be.

Pierce kisses my clit in between licks, and the sensation is one I've never felt before. I sigh, feeling more comfortable with him then with Serena, even though her technique was better. I hesitate before I make a sound, though, unsure if the rules still apply, and Hugh must realize this.

"You can make noise with us," he whispers to me, before leaning over the table to take one of my nipples in his mouth.

Which is a good thing, because I don't think I'm going to be able to keep quiet much longer.

Pierce forgoes the kisses for quick licks of every place he can reach before plunging his tongue inside me. I groan then, and again when he replaces his tongue with his fingers. He stands, thrusting two fingers inside me as he smiles down at me. With his other hand, he reaches for my breast, massaging it roughly.

"My turn," Hugh announces, lifting his head from my other breast. Without a word to me or each other, they switch spots so quickly I think I might be imagining things until Hugh begins to tongue me.

Oh, he's good.

Long, slow strokes of his tongue, beginning with my ass and all the way up, stopping to plunge his tongue inside me, stopping again to have a suck of my clit. By his third trip, I'm beginning to wonder if I'll be allowed to come and that's before he begins with my anus...

Ever since the first night at Tia's with Colin, I've found my ass to be an effective erogenous zone, and Hugh takes full advantage of my willingness. His tongue slowly circles, pressing against the pucker. When he makes the return trip back to my clit, he leaves his finger slowly probing my ass, pushing its way in and continuing to thrust as he licks and sucks my clit. I push my pussy hard against him, feeling the beginning of an orgasm.

"Oh, God," I can't help but cry out and that's when he stops.

"Sorry, love," he says with real regret in his voice. "Can't do it."

"Please," I beg. I don't like to beg. I'm used to telling them what to do, not begging for them to do it. But it's obvious I'm not in charge here as Hugh and Pierce both hop down off the platform.

For the first time I notice what the others are doing.

Serena has shed her dress and I was right, she's not wearing anything underneath. She's standing in front of my husband and Mahak has his hand buried between her legs. As I watch, Pierce steps in front of her, running his hands over her breasts and then kissing her deeply. Hugh helps himself to another drink and settles in with Dawson on the bench.

Which leaves Tandy and Will.

"How are you liking my little party?" Will asks kindly as if I'm not lying on his billiards table, hot and horny and panting for someone to finish the job.

"It's fine," I snap and he smiles.

"You're a little frustrated, aren't you? I apologize for that, but everyone gets to have a taste, you know. You're like my birthday cake and Serena was right, you do look delicious. I think it might be time for my birthday present." He runs his hand down my belly and plunges two fingers inside me roughly. I gasp and instinctively raise my hips as he thrusts into me. "I'm going to fuck you, you see. Do you think you might like that?"

"Yes," I say softly, wanting it now, but knowing I'm going to have to wait for it.

"I'm going to tie you to this table and then fuck you hard. Do you like it hard?"

"Yes," I manage with difficulty, only able to focus on his fingers fucking me.

"Does she like it hard?" he calls to Mahak. I look over to see Serena has Mahak's pants open and her hand inside stroking him.

"She does. She loves it," my husband says harshly.

"Are you going to like watching me fuck her? While Serena fucks you? Do you think you might like that?"

Mahak doesn't answer. "I'm not going to fuck him right away," she says, drawing out her hand. "He's going to make me come first with that tongue of his."

For the first time, Tandy speaks. "I didn't get a turn."

"No, you didn't my love," Will turns to her. "Who would you like?"

I think for sure she's going to pick Mahak, but she surprises me when she points her glass at me. "Her."

Will dramatically steps back. "I'll be happy waiting. Go ahead."

I watch suspiciously as Tandy steps onto the platform and stares at me. "Can I have a fresh drink, please," she asks softly. Hugh jumps to attention and refills her glass. "Lots of ice please." She absentmindedly puts her hand on my pussy as she waits, stroking me idly with a finger. She doesn't meet my eyes and that bothers me like I'm there as some sort of plaything for her.

I guess I am.

I'm letting all of these strangers touch me, play with me as my husband – as the rest of them – watch. It's slightly kinky, kind of perverted and really exciting as hell. I glance over to see what Mahak thinks of it only to find him on his knees in front of a naked Serena. Her head is thrown back and both hands are pressed against the back of Mahak's head. She's clearly enjoying herself. I can only guess what his tongue is doing to her pussy. I don't need to guess because I've been the recipient of it myself.

Am I jealous? Does it bother me to see Mahak do that to another woman? I'd be lying if I said I didn't have a surge of *something* swell up inside me, but I'm too preoccupied to try and figure it out this minute. I do have to admit it's kind of exciting to see Serena enjoy herself at the hands of my husband.

She sees me watching and gives me a ghost of a smile. "You are one lucky bitch."

I grin at her. "I know. And he's all mine."

"Lie back, please."

I'm so busy watching Mahak and Serena that I've almost forgotten about Tandy. Almost.

I comply, my attention on her now, even though Serena's cries have begun to cut the air. My breathing quickens again as I wonder what's in store for me.

Tandy has her fingers in her glass now, stirring the ice with her fingers. Suddenly, she thrusts her fingers inside me. They are cold and wet and...I gasp. It stings a bit.

But I don't say anything to Tandy. She moves her fingers inside me, exploring, stroking. She's not exactly rough but she's a lot less gentle than any other woman I've ever been with. I watch her face through half-closed eyelids as she fingers me. Despite what I might think of her, my body is clearly responding. How could it not? I'm so frustrated, so ready to come I don't know how much more I can take.

I fight not to whimper as she withdraws her fingers.

"That's it?" I cry. Is it time for Will? Because I'm more than ready to be fucked right now, hard and fast, with a thick cock. I've had enough of this teasing.

But Tandy isn't finished yet.

She takes a piece of ice from her glass and holds it in her fingers over my pussy. A drop falls onto my bare mound. And then she finally puts her glass down on the table, only to use her other hand to hold my outer lips open so she can press the ice right on my clit.

I cry out. It's so cold it's painful, but Tandy doesn't take it away. Instead, she rubs it around my clit so the pain mixes with pleasure.

"Ah!"

Tandy doesn't say anything. Her focus is on my pussy, and that's all I can think about too. She rubs the ice everywhere and I can feel it begin to melt, dripping between my legs and adding to the wetness. "Stop, please," I moan. "It's too cold."

She doesn't stop but reaches for her glass and takes a healthy swig. Then she pushes the ice cube inside me and I let out a shriek at the coldness invading my body. I'm so hot I can feel the ice instantly begin to melt but it's still cold. Then Tandy leans over me and begins to tongue me while the ice melts.

The sensation is like nothing I've ever felt before. To have something so cold inside me, while Tandy greedily licks my clit...and then she presses her finger into my anus roughly, licking my clit at the same time. It hurts but feels so good at the same time. I can feel the ice melting as she licks and thrusts her finger in and out. There must be a puddle forming underneath me, but I'm too caught up in the sensations to care.

Tandy laps at me like a cat to cream, but then she stops suddenly and lifts her head. By this time, I can feel my orgasm approach, and I know I'm going to come so hard that I let out a little scream as she stops. I can hear laughter but I'm beyond caring. "Don't stop! Please – don't!"

Tandy gives me a small smile and takes another drink, her finger still probing. I don't realize she has a piece of ice in her mouth until I feel the chill against my clit. By this time the ice in my pussy has completely melted and this cold is a new shock. Especially when Tandy begins to suck my clit, taking as much of my pussy in her cold mouth as she can. The ice in her mouth rubs against me painfully and I shriek again.

This is something I've never experienced. The ice isn't pleasant but what she's doing feels so good. The room is full of cries and moans and I don't realize it's me until Tandy stops to get another piece of ice and pushes it inside me again.

"It's cold!" I cry.

"Shh," Tandy whispers. Popping a fresh ice cube in her mouth, she resumes. At first lick, with my pussy full of melting ice and her finger up my ass, my orgasm starts to build.

She laps at my clit again with a cold tongue and then begins to suck again with her whole mouth, sending me tumbling over the edge. I come with one last scream, but Tandy doesn't stop until the chill disappears from her mouth.

"Oh God," I breathe when she finally lifts her head. Tandy doesn't say anything, just drifts away from the table and Will takes her place and gazes down at me.

"You seemed like you enjoyed that," he says with a smile. "My wife likes to play. But now it's my turn. Could you stand up please?"

My entire body feels loose as Will helps me off the table. Even though the orgasm Tandy gave me is more than satisfactory, I'm still intrigued to see what Will has planned for me. This night isn't anything that I expected, so I can't be sure I'll be ready for what he has planned. Is he really going to tie me up...?

"You know, I stopped using this table for pool a while back," he tells me conversationally. Leaving me standing by the end of the table, he moves to the side, where he pulls out a cuff attached to a thick red ribbon from underneath and lays it on the table. "I've found so many more enjoyable uses for it."

I watch as Hugh leads Tandy to the other side of the table and helps her sit on the edge, like I had been.

"I'm happy to see others enjoy it as well."

Will moves around the table, with an affectionate smile at Tandy, who pushes Hugh's head between her legs. Almost immediately she begins to moan loudly, which is a surprise seeing how quiet she's been for the evening. I wonder if he's got ice in his mouth. Her cries mix with Serena's, who still seems to be enjoying Mahak's administration from the sound of it. He's on his knees in front of her, with one of her legs thrown over his shoulder and Dawson behind her helping her keep her balance. Pierce is watching everything.

What kind of party did Mahak bring me to? Did he know what was going to happen? And would I have still come if he told me?

"Melissa, dear," Will says politely. "Could you give me your wrist please?"

I wretch my attention from what my husband is doing to Serena. I've seen him give head to Jacey and Wendy, and I know what he does in the bedrooms at Tia's but never before have I watched when I wasn't involved. I'm not sure if I'm enjoying it.

Serena begins to come, crying out for *moremoremore.* Maybe I am enjoying it a little.

I stretch my arm out to Will and he takes my wrist and snaps the cuff around it. I give a gentle tug, and then a harder one. I'm not sure what it's attached to, but it's definitely secure. Will moves around to the other side.

"Oh, she likes that," he says approvingly when he's behind Hugh, as Hugh continues to lick Tandy's pussy.

"I want to watch," Tandy tells Will.

"I'll be another minute," Will says soothingly. "You just enjoy yourself."

He snaps the cuff around my other wrist and pauses for a moment. I'm lying with my chest on the table, arms and legs spread wide and unable to move. I feel very vulnerable.

"I'm going to fuck you in a moment," he explains. "Everyone will watch while I do it. Is that all right with you?"

I glance at my bound wrists. "I don't have much of a choice right now."

Will laughs. "No, not really. You're completely at my mercy. I can do whatever I want with you, and the others will let me."

"Mahak," I remind him.

"He looks somewhat occupied right now."

Mahak has traded positions with Serena. He is standing, and she is bending over with his cock in her mouth. As I watch, Dawson slides into her from behind. From the expression on Mahak's face, I doubt he'd notice anything about me.

I'm glad he's enjoying himself, although I'm sure Serena can't give a blowjob as good as I can. I don't think he'll be finding out tonight though.

"No worries," Will is saying. "I'm sure there won't be anything you object to."

"Are you going to tell me what you're going to do to me?" I ask him between dry lips.

He doesn't answer, but reaches under the table and pulls out a riding crop. "You've got lots of fun stuff under there," I note. "Very Fifty Shades of you."

"I like to think they based Christian Grey on me," he smirks. "But don't worry. We won't get into the heavy stuff tonight. I like to save that for repeat visits. Do you think you might want to visit me again, Melissa?"

"Ask me when you're finished," I manage, unable to take my eyes off the crop. I've been spanked a few times by Jackson and Dominic, but no one has ever gone for any BDSM at Tia's.

I wonder if that might change after tonight.

Will moves behind me and I brace myself for the snap of leather on my bare ass. Instead, I feel his fingers running down my back, between my crack and sliding into my pussy. And then his tongue follows the same route.

I get to enjoy it for only a moment before the crack of leather stings my ass.

Will rubs the spot where he hit me before sliding his hand back into my pussy, fingering my clit. "That wasn't too bad, was it now?" he asks in a low voice.

I shake my head, concentrating on his fingers.

"Another one, then."

I brace for it, but it stings just the same.

"Have you been a bad girl?" Will demands.

"Not really," I gasp as the crop stings again. Will isn't hitting me hard but it's the shock of it I'm fighting to get used to. It doesn't really hurt *that* much...and then there's the way he fingers me between smacks that makes up for it.

This is all new to me, but it excites me. I whimper as he removes his fingers again, and gasp louder as he uses the crop again.

"Anyone that's here tonight needs to be punished," Will says. "A few more should do it."

I manage to glance around the room. Serena still has Mahak in her mouth while Dawson has grasped her by the hips and is fucking her from behind. She's moaning loudly, the sound muffled by Mahak's cock in her mouth. My husband's eyes are half-closed and his hands are pushing down on her head.

Across the pool table from me, Tandy has copied my position, only her hands aren't cuffed. Hugh is behind her, thrusting slowly. Both of them are watching Will and I with expression of lust on their faces. Knowing that I'm turning them on so much makes me even more excited.

"Are you ready for me to fuck you?" Will asked, with another snap of leather.

"*Yes*," I gasp.

"Do you need me to fuck you? Will you die if I don't fuck you?"

"No, but...please, just *fuck* me already!" The frustration is becoming unbearable. Enough with the teasing. I need it hard and fast and –

I let out a shriek as Will suddenly thrusts inside me. He's big, bigger than Mahak and if I wasn't so wet and ready I'm sure it would hurt. But it feels so good having him inside me.

"Do you like that?" Will asks stopping after a few thrusts.

"God, yes! Please, don't stop!"

"Oh, I have no intention of stopping until I've got you screaming," he says.

And then he proceeds to fuck me.

My husband is the best lover I've ever had...until now. Will's cock is huge and his thrusts are so deep and hard it's almost painful, but I can't bear to tell him to stop. I doubt he would. He draws his cock out until the tip is barely in my pussy, then slams into me, harder each time, with enough force the front of my legs will be sore from hitting the table. I think I might get table burn from the green baize covering the table.

All of me will be sore from tonight, but I couldn't care less right now.

I'm crying out now as Will picks up speed. It feels so good. Already I can feel my orgasm rushing quickly through me and I come with a little scream.

But Will keeps going and I don't want him to stop.

He fucks me hard and fast and it's so very good.

I hear Tandy across the table making little cat-like noises and I crane my head to look up at her. Her arms are stretching out across the table as if she's reaching for me, her face contorting in an expression of pleasure. She doesn't take her eyes off me as I feel another orgasm building.

This one is big, and intense, and Will knows it.

"I want to hear you scream," he cries out. Without breaking the rhythm, he snakes a hand around and between my legs, giving my clit a quick rub with his fingers. His touch is all I need to send me spiraling out of control and the orgasm crashes through me. On and on, the waves of pleasure engulf me and I can't help but scream loudly, forgetting that I'm being watched, forgetting everything but the feel of Will's cock inside me.

With an animal-like roar, and thrusts so hard the table shakes, Will comes as well.

When it's over, I can't move. Even when Will uncuffs my wrists, I lay draped over the table, completely spent.

"You were wonderful, my dear," Will says admiring, stroking gentle fingers down my back. "I do hope you'll join us again."

"Happy fucking birthday," I tell him weakly.

Want more? Check out Paige's interlude next!!

Paige

An Interlude

Anna Ellis

Three Birds Press

Paige - An Interlude

J ACEY IS BACK IN Mahak's car this morning.

I peer out the window, knowing I can't see inside the tinted windows but having the urge of a voyeur to have a peek. Not that I'd really consider myself a voyeur, but the sight of one of my best friends hopping into the car of the husband of another best friend, undoubtedly for a quickie, does get me excited.

This morning is no exception.

I'm not positive what Jacey and Mahak are up to in his car so early in the morning but I could give a good guess. It's barely light out but that's when Mahak leaves for work and that's when Jacey walks Frodo, her dog. And this is the third time I've seen her hop into his car. It might be a weekly event but I can't be sure because I like to sleep until after the sun has fully risen.

I can only imagine what the two of them are up to in Mahak's car. And imagining it is what is getting me excited. I know Mahak, I know what he likes, and I know what it feels like to be with him. Jacey is a lucky girl.

I could be wrong. They could be talking, discussing what Mahak has planned for the day or whether Jacey is ever going back to work, or how baby Ben is sleeping at night or how sweet it is that their children Hanna and Max are such good friends.

No way.

They are having sex. Some sort of sex, most likely the type involving mouths.

Am I jealous? Hell, yes.

Because I've been with both of them, and I know what Mahak is doing to Jacey right now in that car, and I know what noises Jacey is making, and what her face looks like...

I take a deep breath.

Ever since Melissa gave us that tutorial about *How to Be with a Woman*, and I got paired up with Jacey, I've had sort of a mini-crush on her. I guess it's not really a crush – I've admired her since she and Dominic moved onto the street, but it was after the morning of play I really started to worship the ground she walks on. If that doesn't sound too stalker-ish. Jacey is a beautiful woman and incredibly sexy, but it's not only that; she's got this inner sensuality that really shines through without her even realizing it. Men want to fuck her and women want to be her. I guess women want to fuck her, too. At least Tia does. And Melissa. And I guess me, too, if I was into women. I'm not really into women, but if I was, I could easily be into Jacey.

I turn from the window, still not confident about what they are doing in the car, and look at my husband asleep in the bed. Is there time this morning?

I return to the bed where Colin is sprawled on his back, snoring. I've never met a man who snored so sweetly. Soft and somewhat melodious, and never ever keeps me awake. Just one more thing I have to be grateful about Colin. Other than that whole cheating thing way back when, he's been the perfect husband.

I crawl back under the covers, curling up next to my almost-perfect husband, feeling the silky dark chest hairs with my fingers. Colin has just the right amount of hair on his body.

"Mmf." My touch stops the snoring and without fully awakening, Colin covers my hand with his.

"Morning," I whisper.

"Hey."

"Do you think I'm sexy?" I ask.

"Mm-hmm," Colin yawns.

"Seriously." I prop myself on my elbow and stare at him intently, so intently I startle him when he finally opens his eyes.

"Seriously. Wow, you're really awake this morning." He blinks a few times.

"And you're not. Probably not a good time to ask." I begin to move away from Colin, but he grabs my hand.

"No, this is a great time. Look, someone is as awake as you are." He pulls the blanket up and points down. I can see the tent-like shape in the front of his boxers and smile. "He thinks you're sexy."

"He'd think Jackson was sexy if he saw him in the morning."

"Don't say that. I told you we didn't do anything. I'm not into dudes!" Ever since he told me about the threesome with him, Jackson and Jacey, I've teased him about his 'bromance' with our neighbour. And no, I'm not jealous Colin had the opportunity with another woman, nor upset it was Jacey. It's just the thought of a threesome makes me wish I was as adventurous as Jacey is.

"I know." I kiss his cheek and slide my hand under the blanket. "Wow. Wide awake."

"Told you you're sexy."

My hand tightens on his cock through the material of his boxers, massaging it gently. But as the sounds of the boys rough-housing in the hall reach my ears, I withdraw my hand reluctantly. "Boys are awake."

"Aw, c'mon," Colin pleads. "I'll be quiet."

"You don't know how to be quiet. Plus, you're the one who indulges them in the little habit of waking us by jumping on our bed."

"Yeah," Colin's sleep-rumpled face is split by another yawn. "Probably not my best move. Now I never get to wake up with a naked wife."

"Should have thought of that," I smile at him and pick myself off the bed.

"You ready for your interview this morning?" Colin asks as he helps me make the bed.

"As I'll ever be."

"Dress sexy," he winks at me.

"What if it's a sexy dentist who interviews me?" I counter. "What if he tries to seduce me in his chair?"

"Are there any sexy dentists?" Colin wonders.

"I'm not sure..." I must look disappointed because Colin comes to me and lifts my chin.

"Tell you what – if you get a dentist that you think is sexy, you have my permission to go for it. Seduce away!"

"It might help me get the job."

"Honey, you don't need sex to get a job. But if it helps...go for it!"

"Remember you said that," I warn. "He might be smoking hot."

"He might be a she!" Colin wiggles his eyebrows and I laugh as I head for the shower.

I have decided it's time I went back to work.

Drew and Theo are six now and in school full days. There's even an after-care program at the school I can put them in so I wouldn't have to rush from work to pick them up at 3:30. There's no valid reason for me to be at home all day. Goodness knows we could use the extra income.

I never intended to be a stay-at home mom. I love the time I've had with the boys and goodness knows raising twins is difficult enough without the added stress of a full-time job sapping your energy. Or maybe it's just my boys! I really think I have the most rambunctious, energetic and challenging boys in existence.

I'm sure all mothers think that of their kids at one time or another. But I really believe it! *All* the time.

Colin has never said one word to me about my return to the workforce. I think he's proud of the fact his wife stays at home with the kids. Even though he'll muck in with just about everything around the house, he's really a traditionalist at heart. But he's always been on my side about everything. When I mentioned a few months ago I was thinking I might like to go back to work, he was as supportive as ever. He really is a wonderful husband. Once we got past his indiscretions – look at me! Calling his cheating on me an indiscretion! – everything was even better.

I think maybe the arrangement we have with the neighbours helps with that.

So I have my first job interview today. To say I'm nervous is like saying Melissa has a healthy libido – a gross understatement. Speaking of Melissa, I still can't believe what she told us about the Valentine's party Mahak took her to, where some of the guests 'sampled' her. I'm not sure of what other word to use. Try her out? Taste? They all had a go.

When we first began this arrangement with the neighbours, I never imagined it spreading farther than our little cul-de-sac. Or farther than Tia's house on Saturday nights. But some of us – Jacey, especially – have really embraced the lifestyle. I'm not sure if Melissa knows about Jacey and Mahak's little car parties in the mornings, but I am definitely *not* going to be the one to tell her! Jacey doesn't even know I know. Part of me wishes I never caught them, but watching what they get up to in the car is pretty darn exciting. Jacey is...Jacey is something else. I know she's the reason Melissa has taken things up another notch – she's so competitive.

I wonder what that says about me; the fact that I don't consider what Jacey does as wrong. She's married and she's sleeping with another man. But so am I. And so are Melissa and Wendy. Because it's the group of us involved in this arrangement, it makes it acceptable. I wonder if it would be different if it was Jacey and someone off the street?

I'm honest enough to admit I channel my inner Jacey when I get dressed for my interview this morning. Colin says sexy, so I go for sexy, or at least as sexy as you can get for an interview as a dental hygienist. It's not much, but my skirt is a little tighter than my old interview dress, and my blouse is unbuttoned enough to show more than a hint of cleavage. Not enough to be inappropriate, but just enough to make me feel a little more attractive than my usual stay-at-home mom style.

I'm feeling a little sexier too, these days. I'm sure that's because I've gotten into the habit of having sex with men other than my husband. I don't think this is a bad thing.

I show up for my interview a few minutes early, which is always a good thing, or so I think at first.

The office is in darkness. I begin to get a little more nervous. It's stressful enough that this is the first job interview I've been on in over ten years, and now no one is here. The interview is scheduled for nine-thirty, which gave me time to drop the boys off at school and make the ten minute drive to the medical building. I made it with time to spare, but it looks like I'm the only one.

Dr. Jake Brownstein, Dental Surgeon.

I check the name on the door to make sure I have the right place. I had been a dental hygienist in my past, pre-kids life and it seems natural to go back to what I know. I liked my job. I just liked being home with my kids a little more.

On my last visit to the dentist, my former boss, Phil Epps, asked whether I'd ever consider going back to work because he needed a hygienist. That had been four months ago. It had taken me that long to get my head around the concept, but I'm there now. I'm ready to move forward. Unfortunately, by the time I'm ready, there's no longer an opening at my old work. Luckily, Phil had put me in touch with Dr. Brownstein, who has a practice in the same medical building and needs a new hygienist. And so here I am.

But it doesn't look like Dr. Brownstein is.

I knock politely and wait. I call the number on the door from my cell – no answer. My interview time comes and goes and nothing. No one shows up. Self-doubt rushes over me. Finally I bang loudly on the door, more out of frustration than anything. I'm just about to walk away when it opens.

"I have an interview, don't I?" The man who opens the door is tall and broad and boyish, with dimples in both cheeks and a head full of curly brown hair.

"You do." I can't check the annoyance in my voice, which doesn't make for a good start for the interview.

"You're my interview?" he asks with surprise.

"Do you have a problem with that?" I ask rudely. Late for the interview *he* set up, and now insulting me? So much for returning to work. And for my pathetic attempt to be sexy. "Is it my age? Or the fact I'm a stay-at-home mother? Because I still have more experience –"

Dr. Brownstein raises his arms in surrender and cuts me off. "Absolutely not," he says, with a huge smile showcasing the dimples to their best advantage. "I can't imagine having any sort of problem with you. Your age is perfect and I really like Mom's, especially MILF's..." he trails off and I have a feeling that last part sort of popped out. "Not that I'm calling you a MILF. I mean, I am, but I shouldn't, even though you totally are. But – shit, can we start over?"

What kind of idiot...? But then I take a good look at this Dr. Jake Brownstein, and decide it might be worth giving him another chance.

Hello, sexy dentist.

His shoulders seem to fill the doorway, tapering to a narrow waist and his black T-shirt seems to hug his chest in a very undentist-like manner. The brown hair is still wet and pushed from his face in an attempt at proper grooming, but a few rebellious curls droop onto his forehead. Wearing baggy khakis and...bare feet...?

"Hi," I say, holding out my hand. "I'm Paige Lydeamore. I'm your 9:30 interview appointment." It's the bare feet that get me. And the assurance from my old boss that despite Dr. Brownstein's laid-back style, he was an excellent dentist. It's surprising one of the girls at the office failed to mention how hot he was, but I guess when I worked there, I wasn't into looking at men.

I am now. I guess I've changed.

Dr. Brownstein takes my hand with a grateful smile. Am I imagining that it is also an admiring smile? Is he really checking me out? Because I'm checking *him* out, but trying not to be too obvious about it. He apparently has no qualms about being obvious.

He called me a MILF.

"Again—so sorry!" he says. "I rode to work today and was grabbing a quick shower. Plus, I have the music too loud when there are no patients. My office manager called in sick today, along with my other hygienist so I'm solo. I managed to rebook the appointments I had this morning but I forgot about calling you." He smiles at me apologetically with the air of someone who finds life a bit too much to handle. "It's inexcusable that I forgot you. I don't know how I could have done that."

I'm not really listening to what he's saying; having problems focusing on something other than the thought of him in the shower... "If it's a bad time..."

"No, no," he waves and holds the door open for me. "Not at all. It's a great time." His eyes are a deep brown, like melted chocolate and any remaining annoyance I may be experiencing drifts away. Especially with the way he's looking at me. "I don't need a hygienist for you," he adds and I wrench my attention away from his smile. This is a job interview! Try and be professional. "And I seriously need to hire a hygienist. Rhonda's been after me for weeks and I keep putting it off and now Heidi, my regular girl is off sick more time than she's here..." he trails off as I follow him warily inside the office. "I'm really not making a good first impression, am I?"

"Not so much," I tell him truthfully, but with a grin to take the sting away.

"I'm really bad at this. Rhonda usually does the interviews, but she has morning, noon and night sickness with this pregnancy and is finding the smell of this place a little hard to take. Does it smell in here to you?"

"It smells like a dentist's office. But I remember your senses being out of whack when you're pregnant."

"Are you pregnant?" he asks, eyes wide with horror.

"No..."

"Do you want to be pregnant?"

"Not particularly..." I say and laugh when he gives an exaggerated sigh of relief.

"That's great. So great. Not that I have anything wrong with being pregnant or wanting to be pregnant, but my one hygienist is off on mat leave and the other is just pregnant and not doing well. And then Rhonda, my office manager is about six months along...I think there's something in the water here. I should warn you. Please don't drink it!"

"I'll be sure to bring my own bottle."

Dr. Brownstein smiles at me, with dimples on full alert and triggers something in the depths of my memory. He immediately notices my frown. "Is everything okay?" he asks hesitantly. "You think I'm completely nuts and are about to run screaming to the nearest police station..."

"You remind me of someone," I tell him.

"I have one of those faces," he says off-handedly, then takes another look at me. "You know...you kind of look like someone I used to know," he says slowly. "But it's been a long time...."

"I'm sure it's nothing," I assure him. "We're just familiar-looking people."

"Why don't we go in the back and figure it out?" he suggests. "And have your interview."

"Since I'm already here..."

"And have been for some time..."

I follow him through the darkened office. "We have four chairs," Dr. Brownstein tells me, pointing out a few dentist-related things. I'm happy that nothing seems foreign to me. Six years is a long time to be away from something, and I'm feeling prickles of nerves about whether I'm going to be able to jump back into things. How much training would I need? Am I up-to-date on everything I need? How much leeway are they prepared to give me until I'm back up to speed? Is he –?

I'm focused on my thoughts and I don't realize Dr. Brownstein stops until I plough right into the back of him.

"Sorry!" I cry, embarrassed beyond belief. Not only did I run into the back of my possible employer, I manage to somehow grab hold of his ass while I did it! "Oh my God, I'm so sorry!"

"No worries," Dr. Brownstein turns with a grin, showing those dimples to their full advantage. "I should have signalled a stop."

"No, I should have..." I can feel my face flush and realize my hand is still on his ass. "Oh, God! Now who's making a bad first impression?"

"No, it's really fine. Makes up for the MILF comment. And I love being goosed first thing in the morning by pretty women." My eyes widen with surprise. "That wasn't very appropriate either, was it? I told you I'm bad at these interview things."

"You called me pretty," I blurt out. "And a MILF."

"You are..." he says slowly. "But I'm not supposed to say that, right?"

"It's been a long time since anyone called me pretty," I tell him honestly. "I'm willing to overlook anything else inappropriate you want to say."

"Probably not a good idea to give me carte blanche," he says, holding my eyes a little longer than necessary. "But I'll try to use the filter from now on."

"And I'll try to keep my hands to myself," I promise.

Was that a quiet 'damn' I hear under his breath?

And why am I feeling the same regret? Because Dr. Brownstein has a fine feeling ass under those khakis?

Hel-*lo* sexy dentist!

"Can I get you anything to drink?" he asks when we arrive at his office space, nestled between a storage closet and a tiny kitchenette. 'We got one of those Tassimo things because it's the only thing I can figure out. Rhonda got tired of making coffee for me, or me running out to Starbucks down the street. I need my coffee," he adds.

"I'm more of a tea person myself."

"Let me make you one. Or a latte? It makes a good chai tea latte, or so Rhonda tells me. Never touch the stuff myself."

"That would be great. Thanks, Dr. Brownstein."

"Jake. Please."

Is this what job interviews are like nowadays? Tea and instant comfort level with the interviewer, and the added bonus of flirting and compliments? I guess sexing myself up really worked today.

Dr. Brownstein – Jake – busies himself in the kitchenette while I check out his office. His wall of pride is hung with extra-large diplomas;

an Honours Bachelor of Science and one from the University of Toronto Faculty of Dentistry. He graduated a few years before I did.

U of T...

"Ok, here we go," Jake says as he hands me a mug of fragrant-smelling tea. "I think I might have wasted enough of your time so let me get into interview mode here." He rustles through the papers on his desk, presumably looking for my resume. I'm just about to pull a copy out of the leather case I'm holding, when he finds it. "Ok," he repeats, scanning the neatly typed words I agonized over days before. "U of T," he says, echoing my thoughts. "I was there too. In –"

Suddenly his face falls. "You aren't," he breathes, staring at me with a mixture of horror and delight. "You...are!"

"I am what?" Something niggles in the back of my mind, like trying to remember a dream from the night before. It's so close...

"I'm *Jake*. Jake. You don't remember me. I don't know if that makes it better or worse. We, uh –"

"Oh my God!" I cry out, slapping a hand to my mouth at my shout.

I slept with him.

Not only that, he took my virginity. Jake Brownstein is the man who took my virginity.

L OSING MY VIRGINITY.

For everyone I spoke to about it, the experience was either an amazing occasion complete with declarations of love and a sprinkling of tears, or a horrific non-event – painful, not worth remembering or a drunken blur.

I had been eighteen and had been celebrating my first week at university. It was my first time away from home and I knew absolutely no one. I had gone to a keg party on the Friday night with my roommate. I had never been a big drinker in high school so the few beers I had drunk hit me pretty hard and I found myself giggling on the couch next to a cute boy with curly hair and dimples.

His name was Jake and he seemed happy enough to sit and talk to me. He told me he was in his third year and like me, was from a small town in Western Ontario. I had been feeling lonely and sorry for myself all week about how I had gone away to the big city alone, instead of going to some smaller school closer to home with my friends.

And then I met Jake. He was older and very cute, and for the first time since my parents dropped me off at my residence, I was glad to be there.

Jake refilled my beer and we talked, sitting close on the couch to hear each other over the noise of the crowd. He had his arm on the back of the couch, touching my shoulder when I said something that made him laugh, but I didn't feel nervous about him being so close. My mother had warned me about city boys who only wanted *one thing*, but I didn't think Jake belonged in that group.

After being with him for a few hours, I didn't care if that *one thing* was what he wanted because I was beginning to think I wanted it to.

We had progressed from innocent get-to-know-you chitchat and had moved on to innermost secrets and dreams surprisingly quickly. Maybe because I never expected to see him again after tonight, I was an open book for him.

We talked about what we wanted for the future, and our childhood. High school—because it was still so recent – was covered in depth, and of course, we talked about past relationships.

I had been indifferent about my virginity in the past, worried about how I would lose it but not curious enough to make an extra effort to lose it. I had friends from home who were virgins and some who had had sex. I knew it would happen, more than likely in university, and slightly intrigued about the ins and outs of the how and when. But that was it.

Until tonight.

"Are you a virgin?" Jake finally asked.

"Probably the only one here tonight," I said ruefully, glancing around at the throng of girls wearing short shorts and tiny tops. Neither was my style, but the body suit I was wearing under my jeans did show off my breasts to their advantage, a fact Jake confirmed by the way he kept staring at them.

"Naw. There's more than you think. They just hide it because they think it's a turn-off for guys," Jake told me.

"It isn't?"

"No way! Huge turn-on—for me anyway. To be the first one to touch a girl, knowing she's never had anyone that close to her, or make her feel like that...it's probably like what Columbus felt when he discovered America."

"I don't think you can compare me to an undiscovered country," I laughed.

Jake looked me up and down, his gaze lingering on my breasts before returning to my face. "I don't see why not."

"When did you lose it?" I asked him, feeling my pulse speed up from the way he looked at me. "Your V-card."

"Ah. Now that's a sad story."

"You're still a virgin?" I gasped.

"No, that would be pathetic. Not that my story is much better. I met a girl in my senior year of high school and it was love at first sight. For me, anyway. I guess it was for her too, but she didn't feel it was a strong enough love to consummate the relationship. I didn't even get lucky on prom night."

"Harsh," I pretended sympathy.

"Tell me about it! Anyway, Amy – her name was Amy – decided she wanted to go to her wedding bed a virgin. Even if she married me, which she assured me was in the cards, she wanted to be as pure as the driven snow. We both came to school here and I did my best to wear her down. Nicely, of course. Always gentlemanlike, but c'mon. A guy's got *some* needs, you know?"

"So what happened?"

"We made it through the first year. It was tough, physical-wise, but at least she gave in to a few things. Everything but, she said. So I became good at using my other talents if you know what I mean?" I must have looked blank because he wiggled his tongue at me. "Very good, or so she said."

"I'm sure," I murmured. By now, I was sitting comfortably close to Jake, with my legs thrown over his. His arm was now around my shoulder and he was stroking my arm, coming quite close to the side of my breast at times.

"So I endured. It was tough being the last remaining male virgin in the city, but I made it through. I did love her. We made it through the summer. Came back in September. By then I was thinking an engagement ring might speed things up."

"What did she think?"

"She must have been thinking along the same lines, but without the engagement ring."

"What do you mean?"

"I'm sure it was tough for her. I know women have urges and desires..." he trailed off and looked at me expectantly.

"We do. I do."

"I'd like to know about those urges," he said in the same low voice.

"Maybe," I granted, and he smiled, reaching up to touch my lips with his finger. "First, finish your story."

"Really? You really want to know about Amy? Right now?"

"I want it more than anything," I said huskily and Jake's eyes almost popped out of his head.

"O-kay! So here I was, being the dutiful boyfriend and all the while Amy is screwing her sociology professor."

"Really?" I had a feeling it would end along those lines, but was surprised by the sociology professor angle.

"Really. She told me she was having a meeting with him, and I went to pick her up. How was I supposed to know soc profs don't have meetings with second-year students? I'm pre-med. Anyway, I caught them red-handed."

"Poor you!"

"Yep. Poor me. I was inconsolable for about two days and then my roommate took pity on me and took me out and got me drunk."

"And you finally got to have sex..."

"I did. I had some sex."

"Good? I hope so. After waiting so long."

"You know, the first time wasn't great. I was drunk and in a rush and still pretty wrecked about Amy. I know it's not supposed to matter to guys but...I wish it had been different. I would have done things differently."

"What would you have done?"

"I would have made it special for her. I'm all about that these days. I like to give girls a good time."

I stared at him, hoping my interest wasn't completely obvious. I wanted him to know I was interested, but didn't want to appear pathetic. It's a fine line.

But after talking to Jake for a few hours, I knew I wanted my first time to be with someone like him. Special. Experienced, but not a player. Sweet and trustworthy. Older. And cute. Jake was really cute.

But to want to have sex with him just after we met...?

"Do you want to get out of here?" he was asking.

"Where?" I asked dumbly.

"Anywhere. Nowhere. Just out of here. I really want to kiss you but I don't want to do it in front of all of these people."

"My rez room is close," I found myself saying.

"Perfect." He lifted my legs off and helped me stand, and then took my hand. "Nothing will happen that you don't want to."

I looked up into his dark brown eyes. "What if I want something to happen?" I ask hesitantly.

"I might be able to help you with that."

I hurried across the campus with Jake, inwardly ecstatic that it was *finally* going to happen and terrified that *it* was going to happen. But as soon as I opened my door, all my fears vanished because Jake took me in his arms and kissed me. I forgot everything else.

We were on my bed before I knew what hit me.

"How do you get this thing off?" Jake muttered as he ran his hand across my stomach.

"It's a bodysuit so...down farther."

"Oh, really. Well, then." I laughed at the expression of glee on his face as he reared up so he could unbutton my jeans. It was the era of tight jeans – when wasn't it that era? – and it took both of us to wiggle them off. And then with a gentle flick of his fingers, he undid the fastenings between my legs. His hand was warm and I wanted it to stay there, but instead, he pushed up my bodysuit with both hands, stopping to nuzzle my breasts before returning to kiss me.

I might have been a virgin but I wasn't totally inexperienced. And even then, Jake was the best kisser, hands down.

And then, soon, one of his hands found their way back down between my legs. He lay on his side, leaning over me and I curled one of my hands around the back of his neck, running my fingers through his curls. I wanted to touch him, to explore his body like he was free to do to me, but I was nervous. I didn't know what to do, what he might like. What I was allowed to touch?

Plus, I wanted to see what he was going to do to me first.

I really wanted to see how good that tongue was.

But he let his fingers do the work first. My panties were pushed down, meeting the same fate as my bra on the floor and I felt his hand on my inner thigh before moving closer to my warmth. I shamelessly spread my legs and felt his finger push inside me.

Jake wasn't the first guy to touch me between my legs but he was the first who knew what he was doing. He took his time with me, taking turns stroking my clit with his fingers and thrusting inside me. Soon my breath was coming in little gasps and I was moving my hips off the bed in time to his finger thrusts. I had had what I thought was an orgasm a month ago, brought about by the fumblings of one excited date, but it never felt like *this*. *This* was...amazing. Unexpected. I wanted Jake to touch me, touch me more, all over and as I felt the strange and powerful sensations build in my core, racing across my body, I wanted him enough to beg for it.

"Please, please," I half-sobbed as he increased the pressure and speed of his finger on my clit.

And then it hit. I felt like I was flying, spinning out of control, and I realized I had shouted his name as I came. Tingles and shivers wrought my body and Jake slowly took away his hand.

"You like that?" he asked with a satisfied smile.

"Oh, God," I gasped.

"Let me get a condom," he said, making a move to roll off the bed, but I grabbed his arm. "No, wait. I want to..." I pushed him down on the bed and crawled down the length of his body to where his penis reared up, frighteningly large for a nervous virgin, but mouth-watering for a hungry me.

"What..." Jake began, his body tensing as I took him in my hands, and licked the tip. "Oh, God," he breathed as I took him in my mouth.

I had been initiated in the art of blow jobs months ago but only succeeded once, and that had been over too quick for me to have any fun. This time I was able to take my time with Jake; slowly and languidly moving my mouth along his thick shaft, twirling my tongue around his tip and smiling when I felt his body jerk. I sucked him as hard as I could and I scraped my teeth along his length. I played with him for long minutes, and it was so much fun. Never before had I felt so powerful with a man.

But it wasn't long before he came in my mouth with a gasp.

"You're so good at that," he told me admiringly as I lifted my head.

"I know," I said smugly.

"But I'm not going to be able to...not right away."

"I'm sure we can find something else to do while we wait," I said, lying back against my pillows and parting my legs expectantly. Jake laughed.

"This is why virgins are so much fun," he said.

Jake moved down the bed and put his hands on the inside of my thighs, bending my knees before spreading them apart. I resisted the temptation to pull them together as last minute jitters hit. What was I doing? How could I suggest such a thing? No one had ever performed *oral sex* on me. Gone down on me. Ate me out. Gave me pleasure with their tongue. I don't even know what to call it! And I definitely didn't know what to expect. A few licks, and then was it over? Will I come right away? Will I come at all? I've had plenty of orgasms – most were self-induced – but nothing like this.

"You've done this before?" I asked in a quavering voice.

"Of course. You're in good hands," he promised and lowered his head.

I felt Jake's breath before he touched me. And then his finger, stroking the coarse hair between my legs before darting between my lips to explore my wetness. His thumbs spread me apart. I held my breath as I felt his tongue flicker against me like a snake. Again and again.

"Oh," I released my breath with a little whimper.

"It gets better," Jake said, his mouth against me so I could feel the vibrations.

Long strokes of his tongue, lapping me like cat to cream. I spread my legs wider, opening myself even more to him. I was wet already but the sensation of his mouth and hot breath against me was like nothing I'd ever experienced. And then he started with my clit...

I was fourteen when I first discovered that such a tiny part of my body could give me such extreme pleasure and it had been a favourite of mine ever since. But now I was discovering a tongue against a clitoris could be something even better.

Jake circled my little pleasure bud between flickers of his tongue. It felt so good I couldn't stop myself from moaning, even though there was the possibility of someone hearing. I couldn't help it. And I couldn't help pushing my pussy against Jake's face. He gathered me even closer. I could hear my quiet moans and whimpers and cries becoming louder in the room, along with the slick sounds of Jake invading my wetness.

Jake was using his fingers now, stroking me as he worried me with his tongue. Suddenly I felt the hotness of his mouth as he surrounded my clit before sucking hard at the same time he thrust a finger inside me.

I cried out.

He kept sucking and licking as he pushed another finger inside, thrusting faster along with his tongue. I could feel something building in my core again and I couldn't stop myself from making noises, noises I didn't want anyone to hear but I couldn't bear to keep quiet. The sensations raced through me, overwhelmed me, making me forget everything but the feel of Jake's mouth on me. He sucked one last time, and I went rigid, my hands tangled in his hair, pushing him deeper as my orgasm hit, rushing through me with the strength of a tidal wave, leaving me weak and breathless.

"I hope no one heard you," Jake said with a grin as he lifted his head.

"I couldn't care less," I told him weakly. I watched as he got up from the bed, heading for his pants.

"Is that it...?" I asked with dismay.

"I'm not finished with you," Jake said, holding up the foil wrapper he took from his wallet. "Is that okay? You still okay?"

I nodded as I watched him roll the condom over his cock. The cock I had in my mouth. The cock I wanted inside me, right now. So badly.

Sheathed for protection, Jake returned to my bed and climbed on top of me. He kissed me and I could taste myself on his lips, his tongue. I wrapped my arms around his shoulders as he positioned himself between my legs. I felt his cock, hard and thick again, push against me, looking for a way to get in. I spread my legs as much as I could, having a brief moment of fear when the tip was against my opening.

"Okay?" Jake asked one last time.

I nodded my head against his shoulder, hoping it wouldn't hurt too much.

Pushing, pressure, a brief flash of pain and then it was over. And then it began.

Jake moved slowly, gently inside me at first, but soon it wasn't enough. My hands moved from his shoulders, down his back until I was grasping his firm ass.

"You okay?" he asked.

"More," I gasped.

"Okay then."

He reared up, propping himself on his forearms above me as he started to move. And I started to move with him, bracing my feet on the bed as I matched his thrusts.

"Am I doing all right?"

"You're doing awesome," he told me proudly. And then he scooped up my ass with his hands, pressed me against him. Harder and faster and I couldn't catch my breath.

"Is it too hard?" he asked with difficulty.

"No, good. It feels so good."

I wrapped my legs around his hips and hung on as Jake really began to move. If I had known my first time would be like this, I would have done it a long time ago!

Slowly, my insides began to tighten once more, like the beginning of an orgasm but I wasn't hopeful. I doubted I would be able to come my first time, especially not for a third time in one night! I was lucky it didn't hurt, that it felt so good. But the feeling persisted, and continued to grow as Jake continued to thrust, hard and fast, his thick cock filling me with a pleasurable ache.

I looked up at Jake, his hair hanging off his forehead, fully focused on fucking me. And I was focused on how good it felt, less intense than before, but no less pleasurable.

"Please don't stop," I begged, my hands pressed against his ass. "I think I'm going to come, I'm going to come, I'm –"

And then I was coming, arching up as I cried out, again and again as Jake slammed into me, again and again. Suddenly he stiffened against me, and with a low groan that sounded like a growl, emptied himself into me and collapsed.

"Oh my God," I gasped, running my hands along his back, comfortable even with his full weight on me. I had sex! And I came for the first time.

I was no longer a virgin.

"Yeah," Jake muttered, not even stirring.

"That was amazing!"

"Yeah…"

"Can we do it again?"

This time he lifted his head with a grin. "Give me a bit," he said. And then he fell asleep, still inside me.

I left Jake lying on top of me for as long as I could but finally the need to breathe took precedence and I started pushing his shoulder.

"Ok, I'm up," he mumbled. He rolled off me, his back to the wall and I wiggled to give him more room, lying on my side so that we were looking at each other.

"Hi," I said shyly.

"You okay," he asked with concern.

"Better than okay!"

"You sure that was your first time?" Jake asked skeptically.

"As far as I know it was. And I think I'd know."

"It's just that – I guess I've only been with one other virgin and I didn't really know what I was doing then."

"You seem to know what you're doing now."

"So do you." He kissed me then, long and slow, and I inched closer to him. "Uh uh. Not again."

"Why not?" I pouted.

"There are limits. But that's not saying we can't see each other again," he said hopefully.

"I'd like that," I told him.

"I would too. But not again tonight, not after that!" He laughed as I shook my head with mock disappointment. "You're a ball-breaker, you know!"

"Not a breaker," I corrected coyly.

"No," he agreed, "you didn't break a thing."

He climbed out of my bed and I watched him get dressed before I realized I should probably put on some clothes myself. And possibly pick up my underwear and bra before my roommate got home.

I was no longer a virgin.

I LOOK AT JAKE and can tell he's thinking the same thing I am.

"That was you," I manage, through the haze of memories.

"That was the best blow job I've ever had," Jake says.

Instantly my face heats up, much like the warmth that's developed between my legs. "Thanks, I guess."

"Seriously, I think about that night all the time. No one..." he trails off when he notices how uncomfortable I am. "Sorry. Inappropriate again."

"It's okay. It's just that..." I trail off as well. How can I tell him that night had been the basis for so many fantasies for me as well? I love Colin and we have a pretty great sex life, but sometimes when he's making love to me, it's the thought of Jake I go back to, and that innocent, uninhibited virgin I once was. It's only been in the last few years I've rediscovered that side of myself, thanks to the arrangement with the neighbours.

"I get it," Jake says. "But what happened? I thought we were meeting for coffee the next day?"

"I was there but you never showed up."

"No, you didn't. I spent over an hour waiting for you!"

"You couldn't have!" Then I pause. "Where did you wait for me?"

"In front of the residence. On the bench out front – I sat and waited for an hour. I finally went up to your room but you weren't there."

"I was waiting for *you* – at the Coffee Time on the corner where we said we'd meet!"

"No, I said I'd pick you up."

"No you didn't!" Our voices rise as we argue. Not that it matters what happened so long ago, who said what, who didn't show up.

But it does. I had been filled with regret and disappointment and anger about never seeing Jake again. Thinking he blew me off, that it hadn't mattered to him. Thinking I had been nothing but a one-night stand. He took my virginity but I didn't matter one little bit to him.

It took me a long time to get over that. It wasn't until I met Colin.

"I did too!" Jake insists. "I had just taken your virginity and felt like I should be a gentleman! I was picking you up."

"I don't remember anything about you picking me up!"

"Afterward, when I was leaving I said I'd pick you up at 1 pm!"

"I only heard the Coffee Time at 1 p.m.," I say with dismay. All those years of thinking Jake blew me off, all those times looking for him around the school and afraid of what I'd say if I saw him? Of being devastated my first time ended in heartbreak?

I'm not sure how long we might have argued if I hadn't given in. "I didn't hear that," I say sadly. "But it was a long time ago. It doesn't matter."

But it does matter. Knowing he had been there, waiting for me, helps relieve some of the regret. A lot of regret. So much that I stop remembering how I felt the next day and remember what it was like when we were together.

"It was a long time ago," he agrees. "We were – I was a lot younger then."

"Are you saying you don't have the same stamina now?" I ask with a twist of a smile.

"I'm not saying that at all," he retorts, with a flash of dimple. "I seem to recall I needed quite a bit of stamina with you. And that *was* the best blow job I've ever got," he says in a rush.

"Oh! Thanks. I guess. I'm glad you liked it." I glance down at my hands. Colin always compliments me on my technique, as does Mahak. With Mahak, I am probably the best blowjob he's gotten because of Melissa's refusal to do so. Unless Jacey has returned the favour.

I'm guessing she has.

I wonder if I give a better blowjob than Jacey? She might have more experience but I'm pretty damn good if I do say so myself.

"I don't mean to embarrass you," Jake says gently.

"It's okay. It's just something nice girls aren't supposed to enjoy doing. Even though I do," I add defensively.

"I'm – glad. It's always a bonus when you enjoy something like that."

"If I recall correctly, you were also quite talented," I say coyly.

"Yeah, well, I think some things improve with age."

There is no denying the heat between my legs now. The only problem is how far I'm prepared to let this go. It's harmless flirting right now, but I think – I'm not positive – but I think Jake wants to take it farther.

Who am I kidding?

He wants to fuck me. The way he's looking at me, the way he's talking. The lack of a wedding ring.

And what about me? Maybe...

Who am I kidding? I was attracted to him the moment he opened the door, even if he had been late for my interview. And then when I found out I not only I knew him – knew him intimately – but had one of the best sexual experiences of my life with him; well, I can't really explain how excited I've become. The memories of that night alone have kept me company on many a time. The chance to relive that...

Yes, I do want to fuck him. Quite badly actually.

And Colin said to go for it.

He said if the interview was with a sexy dentist, then I was to go for it. I'm sure if I ask him to reiterate, he might change his mind, but I cling to the thought he said to go for it.

"So," Jake says, finally returning his attention to my resume on the desk before him like this is nothing more than a simple job interview. "Going back to work?"

"My kids are in school. I thought I needed a distraction."

"And you want me to be that distraction? Working for me," he corrects with a sly grin.

There's nothing simple about this.

"I had no idea it was you I'd be working for," I say. "You might be a distraction."

"You think so?"

"Maybe."

Another pause. "Are you still married?" he asks.

"I am. Colin. I met him at U of T. After you. We have an open marriage," I blurt out. Why did I tell him that? And do we? The neighbours are one thing but outside the street – Colin and I have never talked about that. The matter has never come up. I know he was joking about what he said this morning, but...what would he say about this?

He cheated on you, a little voice in my head reminds me.

"You do?" Jake stammers. "Open marriage? I've heard about them but never...not that it's anything strange." He fights to regain his cool.

"Well, sort of," I concede, unsure of what Colin would call it. "It's complicated."

"So you..."

I shrug my shoulders. "If the situation arose, I guess."

I wonder what else is arising?

"Would this be a situation?" Jake asks bluntly.

"It might be." What else could I say? That uninhibited virgin from long ago is rearing her head and there isn't much I can do to stop her. Nor did I want to.

Jake pushes back his chair and is around his desk before I have a chance to react or rethink my decision.

And then he pulls me to my feet.

Interview over.

For someone who grabs me so impulsively, Jake's kisses are slow and careful. It's like he counts to ten before he kisses me, but I know he didn't because he wouldn't have got to three. His arms go around me but I can only grab the front of his shirt before he pulls me to him. We don't kiss for long – both of us are ready for much more than a simple make-out session. Before long, the buttons on my blouse are open and Jake has pushed my breasts over the top of my bra cups because he can't figure out the clasp. His mouth finds my nipple, already hard. I shrug my arms out of my blouse and drop it on the floor and try my best to take off my bra without disturbing him.

No luck.

"Take off all your clothes," Jake orders. He's already pushed up my skirt. I'll never be able to get the wrinkles out.

I obey, taking off my bra and stepping out of my skirt in record time, leaving me standing in his office wearing only my underwear. There's no time to think of how awkward this is, or wonder if my panties are sexy enough because Jake pulls them down himself and then pushes me onto the edge of the desk, pushing my legs apart so he's standing between them. His mouth finds my breast again and his hand is between my legs.

I gasp as he pushes a finger inside me, and then two. I'm already wet and he finger fucks me before targeting my clit with his fingers, rubbing it roughly and sending tremors through my body.

I want more and I push his head away from my breast.

Jake kneels between my legs and spreads them even wider. "I still remember what you taste like," he mutters. Like when he kissed me, he slowed his frantic pace. He begins to lick me slowly and methodically, plunging his tongue inside me before circling my clit, flickering touches that have me gasping. I lean my arms back on the desk and widen my legs even more. Jake throws one of my legs over his shoulder and dives in deeper.

His mouth finds my clit and he sucks it hard. I cry out then, and he plunges his fingers into me again. He fucks me hard with them as he sucks my clit and I know I can't take much more.

"Oh, God! More, please, more!" I cry as I push his head deeper. Then my cries turn to a scream as I come hard and fast, so unexpected that I kick over a chair as the orgasm washes over me.

"Oh my God," I manage weakly as Jake lifts his head. "That was so fast."

"Don't worry. I'm not done with you," he tells me, pulling me off the desk and into one of the examining rooms. I can only stand limp beside him as he fumbles with the controls of the chair, reclining it so it's more than a couch than a chair.

"Sorry," he apologizes as he pulls off his pants. "It's all I've got."

I'm not complaining.

Jake lies on the chair and motions for me to climb aboard. But when I do, he shakes his head. "No. This way."

He positions me so I'm straddling him with my head over his cock. 69.

Something I haven't done in years.

It's never been my favourite position but I'm game if it allows me a taste of his cock as he fucks me with his tongue. Jake is as good as Mahak.

We barely fit in the chair but I'm not about to argue. I grab his thick shaft as it juts up, stroking it experimentally. Jake doesn't wait until I take it in my mouth before he's licking me again, long, strong strokes from my clit to my ass, stopping to thrust inside me before teasing my clit.

It's going to take me longer to come this time, but not much.

I prop myself on my arms as I take the head of his cock in my mouth, swirling my tongue around the tip before slowly lowering my head to take it all in. Jake has just the right amount of length and more than enough in girth. Already I can feel my muscles tensing, imagining what it will feel like to have him inside me again.

Jake's hands are on my hips, positioning my pussy over his waiting mouth, teasing me with flickers of his tongue so I'm ready to grind myself against him, but can't move. Tiny flicks, leading to long strokes and then sucking. I cry out, my mouth full of him as I move my head up and down.

His tongue is back inside me, and then his fingers and I squirm because I want more. I like his thick cock in my mouth but I want him to fuck me with it. My cries are muffled as I suck him, my tongue returning to his tip and he arches against me. Then one of his hands grabs the back of my neck.

"Stop," he says. "I don't want to come like this."

I'm fine with that.

I clamour off of the chair. "My pants," he says, out of breath. "There's a condom in my wallet. I'm still a twenty-year-old at heart, always looking to get laid."

"Well, you're going to get laid," I assure him, rummaging through his pockets. I quickly find the shiny square and rip it open. As he attempts to move, I push him back on the chair, rolling the condom on the cock that I'm desperate to feel inside of me. And then I climb back on the chair, straddling him and lowering myself onto him.

"Oh my fuck," Jake groans.

"Yes," I agree, slowly moving up and down, setting the pace, riding him unhurriedly and smiling at the frustration on his face.

I like being on top – I like to watch a man's face and Jake is no exception. I can tell he's trying to pace himself, biting his lip, closing his eyes with a look of pleasure as I tighten my muscles around him. He grips one of my hips, using the other to rub my clit with his thumb. I ride him harder, but still slowly, my moans filling the quiet office.

I can feel my orgasm coming and I reach up and grab the light over the chair, holding on for dear life as I finally move harder, faster, like I'm trying to race the sensations building in my core. But it takes me and I come hard again, crying out his name. I'm still coming as he grabs me, pulling me down to his chest and in a move I never thought possible, rolls me over with him still inside me.

He shifts for a moment, pulling out as he yanks my legs up towards my shoulders. And then he's back inside, thrusting in me hard and fast.

It's like I never stop coming, the sensations continuing as Jake fucks me and I'm screaming, unable to stop, unable to push back against him. And then I watch his eyes practically roll back into his head as he thrusts hard, once twice and then stops, collapsing on top of me, thankfully releasing my legs first.

"Holy shit," Jake says with a shudder.

"You know I can't work for you, right?" I ask him.

Thank You!

Thanks for keeping up with my naughty neighbours!

When I started Making Friends, I had no idea how much fun I'd have with the group of neighbours and eventually, I knew they'd all have to get their own story. I hope you enjoyed reading from their point of view.

Before you start that, I'd love it if you would leave a quick word about what you thought of Interludes—The Collection, whether on Goodreads or Amazon. Here's a quick link to Amazon!

Join my newsletter to find out more and learn about my characters, and me too! Also, stalking is welcome (The nice kind please!) I'd love it if you'd keep in touch on Facebook and Instagram. Watch for me on Tiktok soon!

Thanks again for reading!

Anna xo

Husbands and Wives

Making Friends
The Husbands
The Wives
New Neighbours
Joe & Jacey

Interludes
Interludes II
Interludes III

Melissa
Paige

Touch

Touch
Touch – Iliya's Story
Touch – Del's Story
Caress
Caress – Iliya's Story
Caress – Del's Story
Embrace
Embrace – Iliya's Story
Embrace – Del's Story

Adults Only

Shared Accommodations
Room Service
Late Checkout
No Vacancy

Office Plays

Lost Weekends

Office Plays
Secrets and Lies
Love After Hours

One

One Summer
One Week
One Night

Fantasies

Gemma
Emmy
Callie
Nia
Malcolm

Peek-a-boo